# THE BARGAIN

## *Paulette's Story*

ISBN: 978-1-944583-30-9

"But remember that reading provides nourishment for hungers we might not even be aware of. How often have I chosen a book at random and found in it an answer I didn't realize I was seeking."

From **Great with Child**
Beth Ann Fennelly,
Professor of English
Poet Laureate of Mississippi

***Written in celebration of the friendships of women. Special is the unique friendship between an older woman and a young girl. There is no competition.***

When I first married and moved away from home, I lived in Holly Springs, Miss., and rented an apartment upstairs in Cedarhurst, one of the town's celebrated Pilgrimage homes. I felt I was living a dream. The old house and its former occupants seemed to speak to me.

The most treasured words came from its owner Leta Belk, kindergarten teacher almost ready to retire. Mrs. Belk and I sat on the enclosed porch at the back of the house many afternoons as she talked to me about her life experiences—losing a child at birth, losing her friends, and the worse loss of all, she said, losing her mate. She was widowed in her forties.

Not all talks were sad. At Thanksgiving she would host a luncheon in that fine old dining room for women who were alone. Out came the fine china, and all the leaves were installed into the giant oak dining table as long as a football field. She did so many good things for others—just like she did for me.

Talking to me in those porch sessions kept me from feeling lonesome in a new town where I hadn't made any friends. Long after I left Cedarhurst, I returned occasionally to visit. She had retired.Her children and grandchildren were living in the "big house." She moved into the 1800s-era outdoor kitchen in the back yard and converted it into an apartment/kindergarten room, and she continued to teach children there a few more years. Her spirit was inspirational.

Now the roles are reversed. In my sixties, I have a brave young friend down the road who challenges me with my horses, while always keeping an eye out for my safety.

She helps me lift and carry, and saddle when my back isn't up to it. She lets me talk, and I listen to her. A newly-wed when I first met her, she now has a baby girl and can't just come over on a whim. In February we took our first ride with baby girl snuggly settled in her backpack. She went to sleep when the horse started walking.

Sometimes it's hard to carry on a

conversation on horseback when the saddle squeaks with every step, but we manage to talk about horses of course—bits, training, temperament, and other things that women talk about.

We went on a little girls' trip recently, and yes, it involved horses. I only hope that I can pass on just half of the wisdom and inspiration for good to Grace Ann Peeples that Leta Belk gave me.

## Contact Me
Read about *The Carving Place* and
*The Bargain, Paulette's Story* on these sites.


thecarvingplace.com
Facebook: The Carving Place, a novel
Email: thecarvingplace@gmail.com

*Part I*
*Paulette Toliver*
*Fall, 1967*

I was never able to attend school for more than a year or two in one place. My parents are flea market people. They went from one flea market to another. We made stops at farmer's markets, tent sales, and anywhere we could set up as vendors. Daddy drove an old Chevrolet with a worn-out camper that fit in the bed of the truck.

Mama and I shared a bed in the camper over the top of the cab. Daddy slept on the couch, and my brother Jesse slept wherever he landed at night. We also carried all our stuff— some glassware, small furniture pieces if they would fit in the truck; but our specialty was books. Not just old junky paperback books, but the kind you would find in a rich person's wood-paneled library. People buy books because they like the author or the subject, but they also buy them because they are pretty.

So, Mama and I went to estate sales and looked for bargains—those pretty leather-bound books or new books that still had the jackets in good condition. Some people just like to decorate with them. I guess it makes them look smarter than they are.

Our books were so nice you really wouldn't expect to find them at a flea market. But we also had some smalls—little odds and ends that don't cost much. We just didn't have room for much more. We kept the books in a metal footlocker in the camper under the couch.

Most kids at school didn't know how I lived, but they knew it wasn't a life like theirs. When I was a teenager, I started packing a little bag; and if I got to school early, I could freshen up in the school bathroom. I knew one of the girls was bound to catch me one day, and if one girl knew, all would know. I couldn't think of another single soul who came to school early in the morning smelling of corndogs and cotton candy.

I bought most of my clothes at the flea markets. Sometimes I got lucky and found something really cute at one of the other booths. I love bargains. Once I got a brand-new pair of shoes. A booth across from ours got in a shipment of last year's shoes. They had never been worn, so that was new to me. I tried hard to fit in at school.

Jesse was tall and strong. He would have been a good athlete if we had ever stayed in place long enough for him to be a part of a team. I could tell this bothered him. He got "that look" when we went to high school football or baseball games.

The year Daddy discovered that there were bunches of flea markets and farmer's markets in north Mississippi, he told us we were going there and stay the whole school year.

Turns out, I stayed much longer.

## Chapter 1—Paulette Toliver

My earliest memories were of this life. I loved it for the adventure it afforded me, traveling across Mississippi and into her neighboring states. The places in our state were as varied as the weather—Gulf Coast at the bottom, rolling hills at the top and the rich and mysterious, flat Delta somewhere in between.

I loved my life for the people we met—most of them. It is magical to sit outside our camp at night and watch the pasture and paths to the woods light up with twinkling lights. Some of the kids from other places called them fireflies. Down here, they are lightnin' bugs.

The fragrance of the camp was made up

of the citronella of the bug spray mixed with the delicious food smells like link sausages sizzling in the iron skillet with onions.

Occasionally when we sat out at night and looked up at the stars, I saw Mama tilt her head back and look at the heavens. A sweet and contented smile crossed her lips. I guess she forgot the bad parts for a moment.

Daddy just sat in an old chair that he leaned back on two legs against the side of the trailer.  He didn't seem particularly lost in thought. He took small and frequent sips from his big coffee cup, chipped on one side. It wasn't coffee. I wished I could see him smile—at me, at Mama, anyone. He must have loved her once. It was hard to tell now.

There were things of this life that I hated, despised—just like that look on Mama's face. Why was happiness so rare for us the traveling family of four? We were bound together by the need to get by.

This life robbed me of friends—the kind that you had known since kindergarten. The ones whose mamas might have been pregnant at the same time my mama was. I imagined that we could sit at their feet and listen to them talk about the record heat wave we had that year in their ninth month when they could no longer see their toes.

I wanted friends that could come to my house to spend the night, diving deep into the covers with an old quilt over our heads. Those friends might have talked about the kind of men they would marry, the color of their hair, the kind of horses they rode, or car they drove.

I imagine that's what lifetime friends talked about. I never had that.

When we bought books, I couldn't wait to read some of them before we put them out for sale. I would carefully take off the jackets, so they wouldn't get soiled or torn. Heaven forbid that I turn down a page corner or write in one. I dreamed of the day that I could have my own books for keeps. If they were mine, I could put pretty bookmarks in them, or even make notations in the margins about a particular passage.

And I hated the hard life that made Daddy drink, Mama's eyes grow dull, and made Jesse anxious to leave. But I did love the books.

Once we get to a new town or location, Mama, Daddy, Jesse, and I would set up our space. If we were lucky, we could plug in an extension cord somewhere and be able to have a fan in the camper at night. Even with the fan, we swatted at mosquitos, making sleep hard to come by. In this part of the South, after the sun goes down, the mosquitoes come out. I always woke up in the morning with a bite or two.

We do most of the cooking outside on a small grill or hot plate. Usually, when we plug in the hot plate, we blow a fuse somewhere, and the other vendors get mad.

So most of the time it was just easier to eat the food that is for sale there. It can't be good for us to eat corndogs, hot dogs, and chili all the time, but that's what we did.

There was the hub of the little community—Crossroads Store—the closest thing to a restaurant for 20 miles or more. It must have started as a general store with basic groceries. Later they added the restaurant part and a couple of pool tables in the back, and when voters allowed beer in the county, they sold that too, and bait.

They fixed plate lunches and featured fried chicken on Thursday night, fish on Friday night, and barbecue on Saturday night.

Sunday lunch was the best.  Church folks turned out after services to stand in line outside just waiting for a table. In the main dining room, Mrs. Pat and her workers moved the tables around and put several tables together to make a serving line. They threw on some white table cloths and it looked just like a fancy restaurant. She had the best fried chicken around. It was dipped in buttermilk and then dredged in flour that had been seasoned with red pepper, white pepper, black pepper, and salt and dropped into deep fat in a big, deep, black skillet.

There usually had a big roast beef that had been slow-cooked overnight. One of the waitresses would stand and cut you a slice of rare, medium, or well-done meat topped with beautiful clear, brown juice.

Vegetables were seasonal, depending on

what was growing at the time—squash and onions cooked down in a black skillet, peas and or butter beans, mashed potatoes with lots of sour cream and black pepper, stewed tomatoes with onions and okra, and fresh corn.

Making the table look like you just sat down at your grandmother's house were homemade pickles served in pink depression glass bowls, and relish made from green and red tomatoes, onions and peppers in beautiful iridescent blue carnival glass dishes. Pickled peaches swam in thick syrup in old china with a pink floral design.

I knew a little about these old glassware patterns since we sold some in our booth. When mama looked at that table, I could see the wheels turning. She was thinking about what we had that Mrs. Pat might want for serving dishes in the restaurant. I sure hoped she wouldn't try to sell her something right there on the spot. I hope she will have the good manners to come back later and bring a few samples.

Mrs. Pat was famous for her signature pocketbook homemade rolls. You could smell the yeast as soon as you walked in the front door. She pulled the rolls out of the oven, brushed them with butter, and put them in baskets on each table.

Since I was never around my grandparents, this was the closest I ever came to family Sunday dinner, because Mama and Daddy never took us to church.

If we had a good week, Daddy let us go on Friday nights to get fish. That was totally different from Sunday lunch. Besides the good food, Friday was the night that the local musicians came with their acoustic instruments and played from the corner of the store. Sometimes they were pretty good. If we went to eat on Friday, we couldn't go back on Sunday unless it was a special occasion.

There was a different kind of Southern food back at the market grounds. At one booth you could get fried pork rinds, plain and barbecue. That was not one of my favorites, but Jesse loved the barbecued rinds. They left him with orange fingers and garlicy, spicy breath for days. You notice these things when you live in close quarters.

There were booths that sold only sodas—

Coca Cola, Pepsi, Dr. Pepper, orange and grape soda, and Fresca if you were on a diet. The drinks were buried in ice in a galvanized tub. They came out so cold that it made your hand burn to hold the bottle.

The man in the booth across from ours was the chair man. Bent and wrinkled, he knew his antiques, especially chairs. From the straight, rigid Shaker chair with their cane seats to the graceful lines of the musical lyre in a Duncan-Phyfe dining chair, he knew how to pick them and how to price them. He could take an old platform rocker with its peeling veneer and refinish it and reupholster it in a beautiful Victorian era fabric, and it looked fit for any mansion in the county.

We got to know the vendors because they usually travelled to the same places we did. Merry Bell Martin was one of my favorite people.

She had a floral booth. Since she was lucky enough to have one of the permanent sites, she was able not only sell plants and flowers but also to grow a few of her own.

Another flower vendor had been there before she was. The ground was good and rich from years of leaves left to compost. The drainage was good, and the light was just right for growing most of her favorites.

Merry Bell had to have one of the spots that had good electricity, so she could hook up her little camper. She had a little tent out back that served as her own little greenhouse.

She was the kind of person that I could sit and talk to for hours. She was a woman of medium height who wore her salt and pepper hair in a casual no-fuss style, tucked neatly behind her ears. A few wisps of hair usually escaped and curled around her face. Her everyday attire was a potting apron.

Just inside the door of her camper was a photograph of a young woman with dark wavy hair, parted on the side. The photo looked like an old sepia-toned print that had been hand-tinted to give it that real vintage look. She sat astride a white horse with a blue plume coming out of the bridle. Her long blue cape was draped gracefully over the horse's hips.

"Is that you Miss Merry Bell?" I asked one afternoon as I sprayed a fine mist across the newly-potted mums.

"Oh, yes ma'am. That was me, many years ago. I don't miss that life, but I sure do miss the horses."

"What life?" I asked, wiping the excess water off the potting table.

"The circus life," she said. I thought I could see a little pride in her faraway look. I think she was remembering her days riding around that circus ring on that white horse, jumping through hoops, doing the death drag on the trick horse.  I was letting my imagination get the best of me.

Looking at Miss Merry Bell now, it was hard to picture her in that beautiful, but tight, little outfit on a spirited horse.

"Do you ever ride anymore, Miss Merry Bell?" I had to squint to see her face with the afternoon sun shining on her and making her look golden. Little dust fairies danced around her head in the sunlight adding to the magical moment. That's what I see when I think of Merry Bell when I shut my eyes.

"Lord, no, girl. It would take a couple of grown men just to get me up on a horse, and I'm sure I forgot everything I ever knew."

"How long were you in the circus, and did

you run away from home?"

"I've got to get busy, Paulette, if we are going to have these violets and pansies potted and ready for tomorrow. We will talk about old times later, OK?"

I smiled and continued wrapping the little pots in squares of purple foil.

## *Chapter 2—Paulette*

Well, Daddy kept his promise. We had been in this location only six weeks when he rented us an old mobile home in the trailer park that sits next to the lot where they have Crossroads Market. It was open the first Friday and Saturday of each month, weather permitting. If it was too bad in the coldest months like January and February, we just didn't open. Having it on Friday let people come and stay for a long weekend, and many did.

We had too much downtime sitting in our cramped truck/camper in between first Fridays. Our mobile home must have been about six years old when we moved in. What was advertised as the "Home of the Future" turned out to be the dump of the past for us. Mama and I spent a whole day sweeping up dead bugs in the corners, cleaning the filthy window blinds, and scrubbing the bathroom and kitchen. From the looks of the trailer, it must have been a seasonal rental with the tenants staying only a few weeks at a time and not minding if they made a mess.

Maybe when it was new the avocado refrigerator, sink, stove and Formica countertops looked pretty trendy. After a few short-term renters it wasn't so snazzy. The blinds were not only dirty but also damaged. Beds had stains that I didn't want to think about. The cushions on the "trendy" couch and chairs were sagging. But all-in-all, I guess it was better than sleeping in a twin-size bed with Mama.

I worried about Merry Bell in her little camper with the tent out back. After eating our frozen dinners on TV trays in our own trailer, I ducked through the bushes that divided the trailer park and Crossroads Market and found Merry Bell sitting under her little awning, wrapped up in an old quilt to combat the chill of the early fall when temperatures at night dropped to near 40 degrees.

"Hey Merry Bell," I yelled before I got up close enough for her to hear me in my regular voice.

"Hey, yourself, Sweet Pea," she said, smiling and getting up from her chair with some difficulty. "How are things over there in the bushes?" She blinked frequently and smiled as she awaited my answer.

"Oh, okay I guess. What do you do the three weeks in between Market days?"

"I read and look at the old magazines that old coot at the magazine booth lets me have…right before he uses them to start his fires. I have found some good recipes in those magazines, and I cut them out and put them in my little wooden recipe box." She nods toward her open kitchen door. "I get ideas for flower arrangements, too," she said like she was letting me in on a special secret.

I notice Merry Bell is not looking too good. I should have visited before now. It can't have been more than a few weeks since I saw her. The color of her skin is not its usual rosy color, and she has circles under her eyes. I notice she begins to run out of breath before she finishes one of her long tales.

"Miss Merry Bell are you OK?" I asked, concern in my voice. "You look a little peaked."

"I'm fine for an old lady," she said, changing the subject.

"Do you need some medicine? What can I do for you?"

"Naw, no medicine, no doctors, no money," she said with a chuckle. "You know when you were here that night last summer and we started talking about my horse-riding days?'

"Yes ma'am."

"I never finished that story." She took a deep breath and settled back in her old rocking chair. I love listening to her stories, and I think she likes telling them. Her voice shifted to a softer tone, and she began her tale.

## Chapter 3—Merry Bell Martin

I made it through the 11th grade when I finally had to quit school to help the family survive. Everybody we knew was poor. Mama stayed home and took care of the kids. She made a little money taking in sewing. Daddy had a government job, and it didn't pay enough to support a wife and three kids. So, that left me to get out there and find a job.

Babysitting didn't pay much, hardly worth your time. The only thing I was good at was working with animals. Our neighbor down the road had an old bay plow horse named Charger. That horse was so old and fat, I don't think he could charge anything or if he ever had.

Mr. Buckley saw me at the market one day and said he'd pay me to come ride Charger to keep him from getting stiff. On the way home from school I started stopping by his place to ride Charger. I really didn't know much about horses, just knew I loved them.

On my first ride, Mr. Buckley showed me where he kept his old worn-out tack in a corner of the barn. The bridle hung on a horse shoe that had been made into a hook, and the saddle and blanket were on an old barrel that had wooden legs. The barrel helped the saddle keep its shape.

Now this was no fancy saddle. It was probably made in the '40s. Dry and dusty, it had sat for years on the barrel. The stirrup leathers had hardened and begun to curl under. He used an old Mexican blanket for a saddle pad. I don't think it was thick enough to keep the saddle from rubbing Charger's fat back.

Mr. Buckley said if I'd come ride Charger and clean his barn, he'd pay me $2 a day. That wasn't much, but it gave me a chance to do something I loved.

After that first day I was on my own. I just dropped my school books on top of the wooden feed bin and gathered the tack. Charger was not always easy to catch. After chasing him around the small lot he was in, I realized I needed to have a different approach. I'd been thinking about this at night when I couldn't sleep.

The next day I stood in the lot with my back to Charger and talked to him in a low voice. After standing like that until my knees felt like they would buckle, I finally felt his nose on the back of my shirt. I didn't move a muscle. He blew a little puff of air as he smelled me. Still facing away from him, I reached in my pocket and offered him a treat. Sometimes I brought a carrot or apple from my lunch—anything I could find that I thought wouldn't hurt him.

When I heard the loud crunch, I turned around slowly and ran my hand over his neck. After going through this routine a few times, he finally let me catch him without all the drama. I led him to the barn and saddled him. Charger must have had some draft horse in him. He was close to 17 hands high, and his feet had shaggy, black feathers on them. A wide blaze of white ran down his nose and over to the right nostril, giving him an off-centered look.

Because he was so tall, I couldn't have gotten up in the saddle if I hadn't mounted from standing on a log or a concrete block before swinging my leg over. As promised by Mr. Buckley, Charger was gentle, untrained, but calm. Even though the gelding hadn't pulled a plough or been ridden in more than five years, he just stood there with me in the saddle. He let out two deep sighs like he was really bored. And maybe he was.

I remembered my second part of the bargain and had to make myself work on getting the barn cleaned out. After riding, I made piles of things—to keep, to burn, and to ask Mr. Buckley about. There was a rotten leather harness, an old milking stool, bits that had long since rusted, just to name a few.

Into the throw away pile went paint cans with hardened paint inside, old feed sacks, broken tools, and stacks of magazines tied with twine. Things tend to get stored in barns and never looked at again for 50 years. These need to be thrown away.

Over the next few visits, we progressed from walking small circles to trotting bigger circles to loping even larger circles. He was so rough I had a hard time staying in the saddle as he tried to stay in a slow canter. I knew I was smiling as I bounced along riding this rough-going, shaggy horse.

"And that's how it started, my horse love," said Merry Bell as she got out of her chair after a couple of tries. "I better get up and start a batch of cookies to have on the counter at the market. Good smelling cookies help draw in customers.

"We can talk about old Charger and how I got to ride that pretty white horse in the picture the next time you come."

## Chapter 4—Paulette

It was getting dark as I left Merry Bell's little camp. By the time I got to the hedge, I heard a rustling in the bushes. I had the distinct feeling someone was watching me. I stopped suddenly and turned. There was nothing but the night around me. Then I heard a branch snap.

"Well, if it isn't little Paulette." I recognized the voice as belonging to Pete Lawrence.

He was about 19, always wore his dark hair slicked back, and was fond of black leather. I'm sure he got that jacket from some of the vendors. His daddy sold animals at the back of the market. Sometimes they weren't cared for very well, and if you believe the market gossip, many were stolen. I made every effort to stay away from Pete and his creepy daddy.

I felt an arm shoot out and grab me by the wrist. "What do you want, Pete?" I said looking him straight in the eye. I smelled his cheap, potent aftershave before he even touched me.

"Oh, I just thought I'd walk you home," he said, forcing his arm around me.

"Just leave me alone, Pete," I said, pleading. I could feel his hot breath on my neck. "Oh, come on girl. I just want us to get a little closer. Know what I mean?" he said winking. As he stepped in front of me, he blocked my path, making it impossible for me to move. In two seconds flat he had me in a choke hold. I felt his teeth sink into the side of my neck as he bit into my throat leaving a bluish mark. As I struggled, I felt my shirt tear at the shoulder.

"Ha, you're just a little whore and you know it," he said, laughing his creepy laugh. He let me go and disappeared into the hedge.

I felt relief and fear at the same time. I had to go home with my clothes torn, my hair a mess, and a blue mark on my neck. Daddy would never believe me that I was the victim.

I came in the side door of the trailer house

and tried to get to my tiny room before he saw me. I failed.

"Well, look a here," he said, catching a glimpse of me. He got up from his tattered recliner and confronted me in the hall. My mother looked at me helplessly over his shoulder.

"What makes you think you can come home looking like that?" he said, with the blue vein in his temple bulging.

"Daddy, I couldn't help it. This guy attacked me in the hedge coming home. I...,"

"Sure, he did. Get in your room and get yourself cleaned up," he said, looking at me in disgust.

I fell on my twin bed and cried until I had a first-class case of the hiccups. Mama finally peeped in my room after it was too dark to see me. I pretended to be asleep, but I could see the hurt in her eyes. She looked older than she had just this night before I left to go see Merry Bell.

I wished that Jesse had been here. Well, maybe not. If he knew Pete did that to me there would have been trouble with Jesse right in the middle of it.

## Chapter 5—Paulette
### January 1968

I looked forward to the summer months at the market. Winter was hard. We were hard-pressed for money, and it was just lonesome. This winter had been especially cold, considering that we were in Mississippi. We would be lucky to open in March or April. That makes for some hard times. Daddy tried to find odd jobs to get us through til spring.

My episode last fall with Pete still haunts me. When he realized I wasn't going to go along with his plan, he told all the other guys that I was a little slut and that he had dumped me. Even though it wasn't true, my reputation was ruined.

I thought I'd like for us to stay in one place

for a long time. Now I wondered if it would be better to move again and give me another chance. I even considered going to community college, but Daddy thought if he didn't need college, I didn't either.

It was about that time that I met Gene Wilson. Gene had just moved into another one of the permanent spots in the market.

He sold odds and ends. You never knew what you would find at Gene's booth. He had beautiful milk glass—bowls, pie dishes, cake plates, creamers, and sugar bowls. All were creamy white with fluted edges. Some customers just liked to collect it. Others bought it to be used as serving pieces.

Other wares included old trunks, a few pieces of antique furniture, vintage toys, and more. His inventory was always changing, where ours pretty much stayed the same.

Even though Gene had this spot at the market, he sometimes traveled to other flea markets and just took smaller items in the back of his beat-up Datsun truck.

Gene was in his late20s but looked much older. He wore his hair a little long and sported a handlebar mustache. He liked to wear a big, wide-brimmed cowboy hat that was stained around the hatband with sweat from working in the hot sun. His arms were muscular from hard work.

I liked to think of him as Gentle Gene. He was always relaxed and smiling. He could be found out in front of his camper sitting in his rocking chair in the evenings playing his guitar. You can hear him all around the camp.

Word around the market was that Gene had been with the first group of Marines to land in Danang in March, 1965, in the Vietnam War. He had come home around Christmas of 1966 on a medical discharge. We couldn't see any physical ailment, but all scars are not visible. He never talked about his past.

One afternoon I was walking around the camp and stopped to hear him play. I sat down on a bucket near his small shack and waited until he was through playing.

"Gene is this a good life for you?"

He combed down his mustache with his fingers as he thought before answering.

"Well, yeah, it is for me.  I had enough of people telling me what to do when I was in the Marines. I like being my own boss. When

I travel to other markets, I see some of the same people and have made some really good friends. There are some good people out there. Then there are some who are not so good."

"How so," I asked. "We have had a few items stolen but nothing big."

Gene thought a minute. "Unfortunately, some people will use their children to steal from other vendors. They will distract the vendor while the kid either steals merchandise or from a money box."

"Got a job for me, Gene?" I asked, pushing a strand of hair away from my face.

"Well, Paulette, what can you do?"

"I've been helping Miss Merry Bell, but she has slowed down some. I learn really fast."

"I bet you do. I don't think I have anything, Paulette, but if I do, I'd be glad to have you help me out. I'll keep that in mind."

## *Chapter 6—Asa Sinclair*

When I finished high school four years ago, I jumped right in helping my daddy on the place. He is still in really good shape for his age. Guess 65 isn't that old anymore. He and my mother farm and raise cattle on the place his parents owned years before.

They have new equipment. Farming has changed. With all the talk of the Civil Rights movement, labor practices have changed. It's a good thing that new equipment has come along, and we don't have to hire as many seasonal workers. In my mind, Dad has always been a fair manager for the families who farmed and sharecropped with us. He was good and generous to the workers, but the system itself was not always so good.

A lot of my friends have gone on to college, either the local community college or one or two state universities in this area. I wanted to go to college but knew I was needed here on the place. I don't blame my friends for leaving this small town to pursue their dreams. It feels kind of empty around here, especially on weekends.

On Friday nights we used to go listen to some music, have a few beers, hang out most of the night. Now Friday nights are just like any other. I'm so tired from driving the tractor, fixing the tractor, mending fences, and dozens of other farm chores that I just want to eat supper, watch a little TV and go to bed.

I heard that this Friday there was going to be some good music at the Crossroads Store. I'll call John Willard and see if he wants to go. John Willard and I have been friends so long that we can't remember when we weren't.

While we had a respectable farm and cattle operation, John Willard Graham III and his family had a real ranch, running about 200 head of registered Angus cattle and some of the nicest cutting horses in a tri-state area.

When I pull up to his place, which is bordered and cross-fenced with five-board white planks, I see by the presence of his black 1966 Pontiac GTO that he is home. That fine piece of machinery was the envy of every boy in our graduating class. The convertible with the bright red racing stripes down the sides also sported red leather bucket seats. John Willard knew he was super-cool in that car, but he was just one of the gang to us. There were a couple of kids who were really jealous of John Willard's good looks and money, but he never acted different to his closest friends.

He must have heard me pull into the circle drive.

"Pull up there behind my car, and we will go in it," he said.

"Hey, man, can I use the phone before we leave? Need to check in with the parents before we head out."

"Oh, sure. I'll go with you." We headed toward the house when I noticed an older-model small, white Chevrolet car parked near the back of the house where household items were delivered. It was missing a hubcap and had a few scrapes and dings.

"Who's here?" I asked.

"Oh, this girl from the market is looking through some books that mama was going to sell.  She always asks if she can go through them before we sell them."

I started taking off my boots at the back door. "Oh, you're okay, just go on in."

The phone, which was fancier than the plain black one that we had, was one of those wall-mounted models in avocado green, hanging right by the refrigerator. I picked it up and dialed home as I was told. Mama answered on the first ring.

"Hey, Mama. We are going in John Willard's car to the Crossroads Store to listen to some music and get a bite to eat. I won't be too late coming home."

Just before I hung up, I could see the girl sitting cross-legged before a pile of books in the den. She wore white pants and had a blue sweater tied loosely around her waist. Strawberry blonde hair was pulled to the side over one shoulder. She wasn't what I'd call movie-star beautiful but was pretty enough to turn your head.

I walked up behind her.

"What are you doing down there?"  I must have scared her since she jumped and looked up at me backward. The books were spread out in piles on the oriental rug in the den.

"Oh, you scared me," the girl said. "I'm just looking through these books that Mrs. Graham is selling. She's cleaning out her bookcase and said Mama could come buy what she wanted. She sent me to see what she had that we might want."

I noticed the piles of books. One pile was for recent, best-sellers like Truman Capote's "In Cold Blood," "Valley of the Dolls" by Jacqueline Susann, and Larry McMurtry's "The Last Picture Show."

"Mrs. Graham has some classics in here too, but I'll have to make a list and then ask her about them. I'm Paulette," she said.

"Nice to meet you.  I'm Asa. Better run. John Willard is waiting on me."

I got in the car with John Willard and off we went.  "Who's the girl?" I asked.

"Oh, just some girl from the market that comes to look through Mama's books that she has already read. Her name is Paulette or Pauline, I think. Why?" he asked giving me a wink.

"Oh, just wondered. She looked nice," I said running my hand over the fancy dashboard of the car.

"She's kind of trashy I've heard," said John Willard, his eyes never leaving the road.

"I'm surprised. She just looks kinda shy." And with that all conversation about Paulette ended, and the night began.

## *Chapter 7—Paulette*

It was near the end of February, one of my least favorite months of the year. I didn't think Miss Merry Bell would be able to keep her booth open next year. She just didn't look like she had the strength. The heat was bound to sap all her strength this summer. I would have helped her out for nothing, but she insisted on paying me a little when she had a good day at market.

"Miss Merry Bell, I'm just going to wash these dishes," I said, noticing that the dishes had begun to pile up in the tiny sink in her kitchen and spill over onto the counter. "Why don't you sit there and tell me some more about your circus days.  You never finished that story."

She was about as reluctant to sit and watch me do the work as she was to tell me about her past. Washing dishes at her place involved running water from the hose into a dish pan and heating it on the stove and then filling another dish pan with cold water for rinsing. So, I knew I was giving her enough time to talk.

"What was the name of the horse in the picture? Did he belong to you?"

"Paulette, you are a nosey little thing. Anyone ever tell you that?"

I laughed and watched her face as she began to relax.

"Well, my circus days didn't last long. No, she didn't belong to me," she said nodding to the picture. Her name was Maybelline," she said with a little giggle in her voice.

"Oh, I figured it was something fancy like Champagne. She's so, I don't know, regal I guess. She doesn't look like a Maybelline."

That little remark amused her, and she chuckled to herself. "Well, don't you think Maybelline makeup helps all us girls look glamorous?" she asked, with a smile.

"I'd been practicing as hard as I could on

old Charger. When the circus came to town, I dressed myself up as much as I could and went to check out the horses and meet the handler.

"What are you lookin' at little lady?" asked a scruffy guy in his 40s who must have been the horse handler. He wore his old jodhpurs stuffed down in his boots. Once black and shiny, they were now scratched deeply, and one heel was worn down on the outside left foot. Watching the man walk, I realized why his boot was worn like that since he had a slight limp on that leg.

I had decided on my strategy. I wasn't going to play the dumb, shy kid.

"Oh, I'm just checking out your string of horses. They look pretty good considering they are on the road all the time. All of them, except that little white mare over there. What's her story?"

"Who made the condition of my horses any

of your business?" he asked, haughtily.

I just continued looking over the horses which were walking nervously in a make-shift round pen.

He shuffled around then said, "If you must know, I picked her up on a trade. Don't think she's got much potential, though. She's shy and skittish."

I waited a few minutes and collected my nerve. "What if you let me work with her a few weeks? If I get her settled and ready to perform, you sell her to me at the end of this circus season…..for, let's say $100."

"I'll let you work with her and see what you've got.  Then we will make a deal," he said. Smiling slightly at my forward manner, he looked me up and down in a way that made me uncomfortable. Then he turned and walked off.

I didn't know where I could get $100, but I'd worry about that later. My parents would not like this deal, but they really didn't care much about what I did as long as I did my chores at home and stayed out of trouble.

I found the handler filling up water troughs for the horses. "Hey, mister, can you get me in free tonight, so I can watch the horse act?"

"We don't make money here by giving out free passes," he said grumpily. "I guess I can get you in a couple of times. Come here about 6 tonight, and I'll get you in."

So, that night and for many others, I watched the circus horses. This was not a big touring circus. Some of the horses were really too old to be still performing, and some were just not well-groomed enough to suit me.

I started coming around about 4 in the afternoon and washing the horses really good. They were all white and gray, so it took a lot of scrubbing to get them clean. The girls who rode them didn't seem interested in getting them in shape or looking better. They just lounged around in their tents and finally got ready about 10 minutes before show time.

I'd seen the handler leave their tent late in the afternoon. I wondered why he spent so much time in there. I thought I might know why, but I didn't want to think about it.

After I gave the horses a good bath and combed out their manes and tails, I tied the horses in the sun to dry. I had found some ribbon real cheap at one of the market booths, and I figured out how to braid it into their long manes, leaving a long trail of color to flow when they galloped.

The handler finally noticed some improvement. I even picked up their feet, looking for anything that could make them lame, rocks or signs of abscess. One day he walked up and down the horse line. "Merry Bell, what am I paying you to clean up the horses?"

"Nothing, sir. I just like for them to look their best.  And Maybelline is coming right along."

"I've been thinking about that. Do you think you could have her ready by next week to do a little arena work in the show? Might be a little something in it for you."

My eyes lit up and my heart did a little flip flop. The next week I began lunging her without a line and teaching her to jump barrels placed on the edge of the arena. She was a little scared at first, dodging the barrel passing it on the side. By the end of the day, she was sailing over them with ease. I flicked my long whip, and she turned the other direction, cantering off real pretty. I was pleased, so I pulled her into the ring and petted her face and neck and put her up on a good note. We repeated that every day for four days.

I finally approached Betty, one of the "trick" riders. "Do you think you could get on Maybelline today while I work her and see how she does with someone on her back?"

She looked up sullenly, smacking her gum. "Yeah, I guess. Did the boss tell you to do this?"

"He said he wanted someone on her this weekend in the show."

"Why don't you ride her yourself?"

"I might just do that." I wondered where that had come from because I hadn't had that thought before it came out of my mouth. "I will still need someone to get on her while I work her. Then I can do it."

"Oh, okay," she said reluctantly. "Come get me when you are ready."

After working Maybelline over the barrels, I moved them to the center of the arena. She cleared them without a fault. I added some ribbon attached to hoops that I tied onto the barrels. She looked at that hard with one ear on the streamers and one ear on me. Finally, she got over one and the next were easier.

Eventually, I added two to the center of the arena, and she cleared two of them at one time, taking a pretty long-strided leap.

Merry Bell took a breath and paused in her storytelling. "Hey, Paulette, can you help me empty those big fertilizer sacks?" she asked, getting up with some difficulty from her chair.

"What about Maybelline? How did she do?"

"Girl, I can't sit around all day telling horse stories. Let's get to work. Maybe I can finish up later."

She turned to face me and looked me in the eye with a serious and sad expression. "Paulette, this story doesn't have a happy ending."

## Chapter 8—Asa Sinclair

If it hadn't been for John Willard that winter, I would have gone crazy. After I got through at the farm, he would come pick me up or I would go to his house and watch TV in their beautiful den with the leather sofa. It was made of the softest brown leather and had wooden arms and trim. There were embroidered long-horned steers on the seat backs.

We watched a lot of *Gunsmoke* that season. Sometimes Mr. Graham would let us go hunting on his place. We had to be mindful of where the cattle were, so we didn't scare or scatter them, or worse, shoot one.

Mr. Graham had some prized hunting dogs—pointers. He would let John Willard and me take out some of the pups he was training to hunt quail. They had instinct but had to be taught to back and hold, and not rush in to flush the birds.

We walked for miles.

"Hey, Asa," said John Willard. "You want to go hang out with me at the store tonight? I hear they may have a little music." We were putting up the dogs and getting them fed.

"Sure. I need to go home and clean up, and I'll meet you there around 8."

We went to the store and decided that we were pretty hungry after all that walking. So, we ordered fish from a middle-aged waitress who had teased her black hair into about a four-inch high beehive on top of her head. I glanced around the restaurant.

"Hey, John Willard. That's the girl that was at your house looking at the books," I said nodding at Paulette who was sitting with her family at a round table near the back.

"Yep," he said, uninterested. I watched them as they ate, never talking to each other. Then the girl got up, I guess to go to the restroom which was located in the back, near the pool tables.

"Be right back," I said, getting up from the table. I hung around in the pool section and when she came out of the restroom, I spoke. "Hey, aren't you the girl I met at the Grahams?"

She looked a little startled. "Yes, I am."

"I'm Asa, remember?"

"Oh, yes. John Willard's friend."

"We are going to hang around and listen to music after we eat. Want to join us?"

"Oh, I don't know if my daddy would let me do that. He's pretty strict on me."

"Well, I'll go ask him," I said, walking over to the table with an air of confidence that I'd never had before.

"Sir, I'm Asa Sinclair. I was wondering if Paulette could stay and listen to some music with me and my friend John Willard. I'll bring her home."

Ed Toliver looked at me like I had two

heads.  "Well, son, I guess that's okay if you don't stay too late."

I saw him give Paulette a menacing look. From across the room, I could tell that he could just give her that hard look in order to intimidate her. Then he turned his eyes on his wife. She just looked down in her lap.

"Thank you, sir," I said, surprised that he had agreed to let her stay.  John Willard was watching this play out from across the restaurant. He winked.

"Paulette, I'm going to go finish my fish. Come on over when your family is ready to leave."

## *Chapter 9—Paulette*

When Daddy looked at me from across the table, it was like hot coals burning into my eyes. He could be so mean. I know he was mean to Mama. I don't know if he ever hit her, but he kept her beat down all the time with his words and looks.

I never remember seeing him look happy. Jesse couldn't wait to leave home. I'm sure by summer he will have a job and be gone. My last protection will leave with him.

While he was putting his stare on me, he took a big bite of chicken and along with it a big chunk of the inside of his mouth. He hollered loud enough that other guests in the restaurant turned to look. I could have melted into the floor. Guess he will blame that one on me, too.

"Paulette, I expect you home early, you hear?" he said, wiping his mouth with the napkin. He pushed back his plate and looked at Mama. "Ready to go?"

Without a word, she pushed back her unfinished plate and followed him to the door. Jesse was already in the truck.

I took my time and finished my tea. Then I went into the restroom and straightened my hair and put on a hint of lipstick. That was about all the improvement I could make. Never thought about meeting up with somebody at the store. I had left home in an old, light-pink button-down shirt. Rolling the sleeves up, I checked myself in the mirror one more time and walked out the door.

Asa was standing there waiting on me.

"Come on, Paulette, let's go listen to the music." He and John Willard had moved to a smaller table, closer to the music. It wasn't so loud that you couldn't talk to each other.

He introduced me to John Willard, who was tall—I'd guess a little over 6 feet. He had dark hair that he combed back with a lock that escaped and touched his eyes.  And they were deep blue. He was definitely a good-looking guy—fast car, family money, and seemingly unattached. I knew he was out of my league.

Asa, on the other hand, was a genuinely sweet man. He, too, was tall, but about an inch shorter than his friend. He wore his brown hair parted on the side. It was getting a little long, but I liked it. And he had the most kind, blue-gray eyes I'd ever seen.

We talked, listened to the music, and I had part of Asa's beer. It was really bad, but I forced it down. I think he had already had a couple. Conversation came a little easier as the night wore on.

The band—a singer, guitar player, bass player, keyboard player, and a drummer—started the first few notes of "Brown-Eyed Girl" now on the charts by Van Morrison. Asa took me by the hand and nodded at the dance floor.

I could feel my heart racing and my hands shaking. "I'm not very good," I said looking up at him apologetically. What I really meant was that I'd never danced before except in my room by myself looking in the mirror. Didn't exactly like what I saw looking back at me.

But Asa pulled me close, took my hand, and guided me around on the floor. He sang the song along with the band. Whispering in my ear he said, "Are you a brown-eyed girl?" He pushed me back and looked at my eyes. "Nope, they are blue," he said as he pulled me back in.

My head was spinning from the beer, his touch, the music. It was a magical night. When the song stopped, we sat down to catch our breath.

"Are you having fun?" he asked.

"Oh, I absolutely am," I said, smiling and still breathing hard. I knew my hair was a mess and damp on the back of my neck. "Oh, Asa, I am having fun, but it's almost 10 o'clock. You better take me home. I don't want to face Daddy if I get in late."

Asa nodded. "I understand. John Willard, you want to hang out here while I take Paulette home?"

"Sure," said John Willard. "Glad we got to spend some time with you, Paulette. Maybe we can do it again soon." He had stood when I did. It was hard to get used to all this polite manly behavior. It never happened at my house.

We stepped out in the night air, which was thick with humidity. I hopped up in the truck beside Asa as he moved things around from the seat to the floor. It looked like a cattleman's truck with some fencing tools in a bucket, wound ointment in a sack from the feed store, and a rope hanging from the gun rack behind the bench seat.

"Sorry about the mess. I didn't know I'd be having company in the truck tonight," he said flashing his lopsided smile at me.

"Oh, that's okay. My brother Jesse's old truck looks a lot worse than this."

"I think I've met your brother a time or two," said Asa. "Nice guy, but I'd hate to tangle with him."

We rode the two miles back to our trailer at the market in silence except for the music on the radio fading in and out. He opened the windows, so we could get some air.

Asa turned the truck off when we got to our trailer. "What do you all sell mostly?"

"Books, mainly, and a few other odds and ends." It was still hard for me to look into his eyes when I talked to him.

"Well, gosh, I should have known that since I saw you going through Mrs. Graham's books that day. Do you like to read?"

"I love it. I usually read the books before we sell them. It's the only way I can escape."

"Escape?" he asked and then looked as if he shouldn't have said anything.

"Yeah. This is not exactly the life I'd like to be living. There are some interesting and nice people here at the market. They make all this bearable. Asa, I had a nice time, but I better get in." I'd already seen someone pull the curtain back to look out a time or two.

"Oh, right. I don't want to get you in trouble. It was fun." He leaned in and gave me a little kiss on the cheek before I knew what had happened. Asa smiled and touched my shoulder as I opened the door and stepped down from the truck.

"Night," he whispered. I knew it was just a dance and a peck, but I'd never met anyone as kind as Asa Sinclair in my life.

I stood there in the dark, damp night and watched his tail lights as they turned onto the highway. Then I faced the trailer and dreaded opening the door. I'd no sooner gotten in the door until I heard Daddy yelling at me. I wasn't even late.

## *Chapter 10—Gene Wilson*

I've got to think of something for Paulette to do tomorrow. I really don't know why I told her she could work a little. I can't afford to pay her. You can just look at her daddy and tell she must have a hard time at home. I just wanted to give her an excuse to get away from that trailer even if it's just for a little while.

Tomorrow I'm getting in a bunch of glassware and a couple of antique tables, the kind made of oak with the ball and claw-feet legs. She can clean up the dishes and polish those tables. That should take her about two hours to do. Guess I can afford that.

Maybe while she works I can clean up a little around here.

All my shelves need cleaning, and the odds and ends need dusting. I really should do it myself, but I'll let her try her hand at making some of the displays look better. I have to keep busy—keep my body busy—keep my mind busy. Sometimes I look down to see my hands shaking uncontrollably.

Right after that I feel sweat start to fall from my face even if it's freezing outside.

I can't unsee some of the images that run through the back of my mind all the time. When they come to the surface, I fall to pieces, just like that Patsy Cline song.

## Chapter 11—Merry Bell

"Well, Paulette, do you want to hear more about Maybelline?" asked Merry Bell as she put a tray of four-inch potted pansies in her little make-shift greenhouse tent. It was a little late for pansies, but some of the ladies in town used the small pots in table decorations for banquets and church meetings and such.

"Sure. You know I do," said Paulette. "Is it going to make me cry?"

"That depends on what kind of mood you are in." Merry Bell shook out her potting apron and adjusted the little space heater in the tent. Her wispy gray strands of hair had escaped her braid and fluttered around her face. Even though it was winter, the temperature was pretty warm for a February night.

She continued her tale.

I thought about letting Betty ride Maybelline in the show that Friday night. The more I thought about it, the more I knew that I could make her look better. She trusted me, took cues from me, and I could anticipate her moves.

"Betty, I think I'll just ride the filly in the show. I shouldn't have bothered you. She's a little skittish, and I wouldn't want you to get hurt."

"Whatever," said Betty as she continued to flip through her magazine without reading a single word.

"Hey, you don't have any old costumes that I could try just this once, do you?"

"Look in that trunk. If they are in there, they have stains or rips. If you fix one, you can wear it. I'll even do your hair."

That was about the nicest she had been to me since I met her a few months ago.

"Great, thanks."

I couldn't wait until I could get Maybelline saddled so that we could work out our routine. It wasn't supposed to be really hard. It just needed to be smooth and make her look pretty.

After making a few laps around the practice arena, I guided her to the center where I'd put a barrel. I took my time and loped her toward it, letting her get her head before she leaped over the barrel. She cleared it perfectly. Coming off the barrel, we circled left and splashed through a little shallow water spot I had made in the arena. It would be bordered by some ferns I had borrowed from the front tent.

I started the pattern again, and I dropped the reins and let her clear the barrel again. This time we circled right, and I ducked my head as she went under a white lattice arbor that I had found at the back of the lot and painted white with sparkling pink glitter.

After a few more circles with my hands over my head, we stopped, and she went down to one knee for a bow.

Friday couldn't come soon enough. I found a beautiful outfit in navy blue with silver trim. It had a slight tear in the side. I decided this was what I needed to help me finally tell mama what I was doing and ask her to help me repair it.

I tucked the costume in my bag and left feeling pretty good about myself. When I walked in that afternoon, Mama was sitting at the kitchen table with all her sewing supplies spread out before her. She was mending a prom dress for a teenager that I'd recognized from school. Daddy was not there.

Sitting beside her at the table, I watched her as she worked. Then I got enough nerve to talk to her about it.

"Mama, do you wonder what I do after school?'

"Yes, I do. But I have a good feeling about whatever it is because you come back home smiling with a bounce in your step. I hope that means what you are doing is good and makes you happy. You deserve it." She smiled and gave me a kiss on the cheek, a rare demonstration of affection from her.

So, I told her about old Charger and riding him, and then meeting the horse trainer at the circus and Maybelline, and the bargain I'd made with the trainer. She seemed to smile as I talked with animation about Maybelline and how good she was doing and the show Friday night. Then I pulled out the costume.

"Can you help me fix this? I can try, but I know you can do a better job. I thought you might even have some silver trim I could add to the horse's blanket or to her mane. Can you help me make her pretty? And don't tell Daddy. I'm not getting paid, and he will think that I am and hiding it from him."

"Sure, I can," she said and bent down to look through the trunk where she kept supplies. She brought up a spool of navy-blue thread. "That's a start."

She worked into the night, and the next morning when I woke up there was my costume on the foot of my bed. It was so pretty. You could hardly tell it was second hand. She had braided some rope with silver ribbon through it for me to use somewhere on Maybelline. I'm sure she thought I'd know better than she did where horse tack went. There were also some silver ribbons with white feathers attached to them that could stream out behind her saddle. I couldn't believe it.

I could hardly wait til school would end today so I could go to the circus ground and start washing and grooming Maybelline.

Thirty minutes before showtime, I had Maybelline groomed to perfection. She was saddled, her mane braided, and she had silver and navy-blue streamers flowing from her tail.

The trainer walked up and inspected her. I could tell he was impressed but was trying to keep a deadpan expression. "Better be good, kid. After the show we might be ready to make a bargain."

My stomach lurched. That could be good or bad. I just kept getting ready and trying to focus. I put on my beautiful costume. I doubt Betty realized it was her old one because Mama had improved it so much.

When the grand entry started, the trainer put me in the middle of the other horses, so Maybelline would be calm. She tucked her nose and extended her trot, looking beautiful and elegant. Surprisingly she wasn't bothered at all by all the fancy streamers flowing from her head to tail.

We exited the arena for the other groups to come in. I patted her on the neck and walked her in slow, big, round circles to keep her moving and to let her relax.

After the trick riders came in, the circus ringmaster introduced us by saying, "This is the debut night for Maybelline. She was just a wild and unruly animal until this kid tamed her in just a few weeks. You can look for her to do more spectacular things in the future!"

When we came in trotting a fast-extended gait, the crowd cheered. I could feel her tense for a moment at the crowd noise, but she soon relaxed. I moved her up into a lope, and we did a few figure eights in the arena. Then I took her to the edge of the arena, still in a lope, and she sailed over the pretty little jumps I had made from some wood pallets.

After going over the first one, our helper added a second jump about a foot from the first one, making her take a longer jump. When she came back to that point, she flew over with no problem.

We did a few more maneuvers and went to the center where I dismounted. I cued her, and she went down on her knees in a beautiful bow. I knew this was not the fanciest routine compared to the trick riders, but it showed me that she had great potential.

I was proud.

I led her back to the stall tent to start un-saddling her and brushing her down. The trainer walked up.

"Pretty good kid."

"Thanks.  It wasn't much, but she will just improve from here."

"So, let's talk about this deal," he said. His eyes suddenly averting mine. "You said you would pay me $100 for her at the end of the circus season. Right?"

"That's what I said."

"Well, I'm going to have to change the terms a little. She's not skittish or nervous after all.  So, my price for her is $500."

I felt my heart skip a beat. How could he do this to me? "She's not skittish and nervous because I brought her out of that. How can you just change the deal?"

"My horse. I can do anything I want to." He was still looking over the gate at nothing and averting my eyes.

"No sir, that's not what we agreed on." I looked directly at him.

"If you are going to get smarty with me, just pack up your stuff. You did a good job with her, I'll give you that.  But I ain't going to have any smart mouth kid talk to me that way. If you change your mind, she will be here til the end of the circus season. But by then her price may be even more."

"Who are you going to put on her?" I asked. It took everything I could muster to keep from tearing up. "Betty? She will have her all high headed and wild after one ride."

"That's it kid. Pack up your stuff and get out of here. And leave the costume. It belongs to Betty and the circus company." He spat and turned and walked away.

I never saw little Maybelline after that, Paulette. And I've never ridden since. I cried all the way home. But I didn't regret one minute of my time working with that pretty thing.

When I think back on that performance and my work with her, it still gives me a thrill. It makes me smile inside. I was just a little country girl, and I did something special. When things are tough, I close my eyes, get on that pretty little mare, and go flying over those jumps with the streamers floating behind me."

## Chapter 12—Asa Sinclair

When you check fences and work cows from horseback like Daddy and I do, you have a lot of time to do some important thinking. I met somebody the other night in town that I can't get off my mind. When she looked up from her plate of food at the diner in town, she caught my eye. I don't think either of us wanted to look away.

I didn't get to talk to her. She was with a group of her girlfriends, and, as usual, I was with John Willard. We weren't at the Crossroads Store, but in town at a little diner that was in a shiny, silver bullet-shaped trailer. The counters were red and white Formica, and the floors were black and white checkered tiles. Best hamburgers I ever ate.

I finally looked away to catch my breath, and when I spun back around on the red leather and chrome stool, she was gone.

"Who was that girl?" I asked John Willard.

"What girl?" he asked, not paying much attention to me.

"The one that was sitting on the other side of the counter? Long dark hair, green eyes, beautiful?"

"Don't know. You ready to go?"

"I bet you can find out who she is," I said, thinking he had connections that I did not.

We jumped in his super car and sped down the highway toward his house where I'd left my truck.

"Hey, John Willard, I kinda hate I've started a little something with Paulette. She's a good girl, and I think she's smart. But when I see someone like that girl back at the diner, I know I'm not ready for a serious relationship. Know what I mean?"

"Yep. Keep your mind on where you are heading with the farm. Those serious things make my head hurt."

He accelerated the Firebird and pulled

out of a curve. Sometimes he scared me a little with his driving in that car. We zoomed down the highway.

The sound of Jefferson Airplane's *Somebody to Love* was coming through the speakers of the car, the windows were down, and the pavement was slick black from a recent rain. It should have been a great moment for a guy figuring out how to be an adult.

Why did I have that funny feeling in the pit of my stomach?

About 10 that night, the phone in the hall rang. We usually didn't get calls after 8 or so. I jumped up and answered the phone since it was right outside my bedroom door.

"Beth Ann Walker," I heard John Willard say, without any introduction. He must have done some checking. "She is Sarah Cunningham's cousin from middle Tennessee. She's here for the weekend." He clicked off.

Well, thanks, I thought to myself. Now I wouldn't be able to sleep.

## Chapter 13—Paulette

I've been working for a while now to get the booth ready for the spring market.  Since it is still the dead of winter in February, it's hard to think pastel, spring decorations. I sat on the floor in the trailer's tiny living room and organized the trunk of books. I put all the classic literature on the first layer in the trunk. These are the leather-bound books that are usually priced from $5 to $50 depending on if they are really special. That means a first edition or something like that.

Then I alphabetized the modern hard-backed books. These were usually $2 if they were in good condition. Last layer was for the recent paperbacks. If these hadn't had the pages turneddown or dogeared and had no writing or markings in them, they were priced from 25 to 75 cents. We usually sold out of these first. Then the second layer sold pretty fast. It took a special buyer to want something from our Private Collection.

I had shopped at the other booths to find items that I could display the books in. I found an old wooden ammunition case that I had painted dark green to hold the paperbacks. We used a couple of different tables to display our items.

On one table I planned to put the hardback books between two old irons that I used like bookends. In another area I would use two candlesticks as end pieces. The Private Collection was kept in a smaller wooden trunk. Usually repeat customers asked to see these. Those customers could be decorators, office managers for lawyers and other professional people, and sometimes just a creative homeowner who was working on their own living room or library.

Mama had some old quilts and lace tablecloths that she had collected over the years that we used for table coverings. I guess I'll be busy, running back and forth between our booth and Merry Bell's. Gene may even want me to help him awhile.

The falling leaves that Merry Bell raked up and composted every year made a rich bed for planting.  She had found an old iron bed in one of the market booths. After putting boards on the sides, she used it to form a raised bed. It always made the ladies smile to see plants in a bed frame.

Mainly, I just plant seeds, transfer them to small cups when they sprout, then move them to 4-inch pots, and finally to 6-inch containers.

I'm trying to learn as much as I can in case Merry Bell isn't here next year. I have a sad feeling this may be the last market for her. She's not really that old, but she has made it on her own for a long time. It has taken a toll on her.

I was working on the booth when I had the feeling that someone was watching me. Turning quickly to my left, I caught a glimpse of dark hair and a black shirt. He turned the instant he saw me looking his way. Pete. Where did he come from?

Just when I start to forget about him and

the incident, he resurfaces. I just kept arrang-
ing the books at the booth, keeping my head
down, hoping he would go away. But he didn't.
Pete's eyes gave away his pretend toughness.
He had to stalk and hurt someone like me to
make himself look tough and powerful.

I saw him pacing around the edge of the
market about the time it was getting dark and
near closing time. I could tell my hands were
shaking and a cold sweat had popped out on
my forehead. Then Pete vanished.

I was stacking up the books while Mama
folded the quilts and tablecloths and brought
them inside for the night.

When she went inside the camper to put
the trunk up, I felt a hand cover my mouth
from behind. "Well, if it isn't little Paulette."

He dragged me into the dusky night away
from the booth. Mama would think I'd just
gone to help Merry Bell or Gene. She wouldn't

miss me for a while. Thoughts were running wild in my head, but I was trying not to fight or panic.

Pete pushed me into his 1965 Ford Fairlane, and we sped off. It would have been a nice car except for the animal crates in the back seat and bedding on the floor that smelled of dog urine and open sacks of food. More proof in my mind that Pete may have been the one stealing the dogs for his daddy's pet booth.

He drove over a dark country road and across an old wooden bridge and killed the lights. It was deadly silent. No chirping crickets, no croaking frogs. I sat as still as I could while he just sat in the seat across from me and looked me up and down.

I knew I couldn't get out the door on my side. He had parked right next to the edge of that old rotten wooden bridge. If I opened the door, I would fall into that deep and dry creek bed many feet below—nothing but hard rocks and sand since we hadn't had any recent rain.

I closed my mind and let my imagination take me away from the moment. There was no one to hear me scream. I had no way out.

That night Pete killed my spirit, my

innocence, my self-esteem. When he was done, he drove me to the far side of the market.

"If you talk about this night, Paulette, you will regret it. You wouldn't want anything to happen to your mama or old Merry Bell, would you?" With that, he started the car and kept the lights off as he disappeared into the night.

What could I do? Where could I go?  My shirt was torn, and I had blood stains on the seat of my jeans. My hair was a mess and the little bit of mascara I had on had run down my face with silent tears.

The little light over the kitchen sink in Merry Bell's camper was still on.  I made my way over and knocked on the door.

When she saw me, she let out a muffled cry. "Come here Paulette," she said opening her door and her arms. She just held me until I quit shaking and crying.

"Come on, let's get you cleaned up.  Who did this?"

I never said a word.

"Does your mama know that you are okay?" she asked.

"No, I don't know what she thinks.  He just

grabbed me and took off."

Paulette poured hot water from a kettle on the stove and made a sink of soapy water. She handed me a clean wash cloth and towel.

"Do you want to call the police?"

"I don't know what to do."

"You just sit here. I'm going to get your mama and bring her over here and we will decide." She walked out letting the door slam behind her.

When she came back with Mama, I fell apart again. I told her the whole story and more about the attack months ago.

"You can't come home like that. Your daddy will never believe you. I'll go get you some clothes while you clean up. You don't want to tell the police. They will ask you all kinds of private questions, and the whole community and folks at school will know. I'll tell your daddy you are staying to help Merry Bell tonight."

I had mixed feeling about all that. I didn't want to go to the police and have them ask me all things that I'd never talked about before, but I also didn't want to have to look for Pete behind every bush or tree as long as we stayed at the market.  Where would it end?

Looking down I noticed a trickle of blood that had run down my leg and puddled in my shoe. "Go on and clean up," she repeated, like washing away the blood would make it all disappear.

After I washed myself, Merry Bell gave me one of her old nightgowns, which hung on me like a potato sack. It was soft and clean and felt good to my hot and bruised skin. She made up a little place for me on her couch and covered me with a quilt. Sitting beside me, she tuned on a little black oscillating fan to blow a gentle breeze over me. With the help of one of Merry Bell's little nerve pills, I finally fell asleep. The last thing I remember is Merry Bell sitting on a stool by the couch, gently brushing my hair back out of my eyes.

The next morning, I woke up suddenly, remembering where I was and why.  It hurt to move. Mama had dropped a sack of clothes on Merry Bell's doorstep with a note.

Just stay till day after tomorrow. He thinks you are helping Merry Bell do some chores. I sent Jesse to school to tell them you were sick. Daddy is working a job in town, so that will give you a day or two. If you need to go to the doctor, tell Merry Bell to come get me.

Most of the day I slept. Then I looked through some magazines while Merry Bell stayed busy working on some plants for the next day's market. I knew Gene must wonder why I hadn't come by to help him bring in plants last night. Just the thought of walking over there by myself made me have cold shivers.

I jumped when I heard the sound of gravel crunching under tires outside the camper. When I realized it was Jesse in his 1965 blue and white Chevy truck, I let out a sigh of relief. He tapped on the camper door and came in; his big frame filled the room.

"I went by the school and talked to the lady in the office. Just told them you were sick," he said. He sat on a low stool with his elbows resting on his knees, looking down at his worn boots. He couldn't bring himself to look me in the eye.

"Jesse, can you go tell Gene I'm sick and that's why I didn't come to help him pack up last night? I can't help him set up this morning either. I'm just scared to walk over there."

'Sure," said Jesse. "I'll go help him. You just rest.  But don't be afraid to go anywhere around here."

"I can't help it. I……" My words caught in my throat. I noticed Jesse's knuckles were swollen, and the skin burst open on his right hand.

Then he looked me directly in the eye. "You don't be scared, little sister. Now or ever. It's okay. Just get well."

He got up to leave and gave me a weak smile. He turned and ducked his head to get out the small door. I was left sitting there in Merry Bell's nightgown with my mouth open. I understood. At the same time, I didn't want to know the details.

## Chapter 14—Merry Bell

I'm just sick about what has happened to my little friend Paulette. She may carry that scar on her heart the rest of her life. I see her trying to move forward—going to school, helping Gene and her mama and daddy, and me. What would I do without her?

I'm trying to teach her about flowers, what to grow, when to fertilize, the best time to prune. I have a cutting garden for some of the local varieties that I sell, like roses, daisies, and zinnias. I have to get a few things from a wholesale place up in Memphis. I don't go there as much. I might be able to get Paulette to drive me up there the day before market. Once a month is not bad.

She has a lot on her for a girl her age. I wish

she could break out of this life—go to college, find a good man, and start a family. She tries to hide her hurt, but I see it just beneath the surface.

So far, I've heard no gossip about her "incident." Maybe Jesse took care of that too. I think Paulette may have a little crush on Asa Sinclair, but I can't see that going anywhere. He's a good boy from a good family. Somehow, I can't imagine his looking for a wife here in the market grounds. You never know.

Guess I'll go outside and do a little work. I can't depend on Paulette to do everything for me. I can tell that it's getting harder for me to keep up this lifestyle. My cousin Clara has asked me to come live near her in Tennessee. I've been fighting that idea for some time now. But lately, that plan is growing on me. I'll see if I can find a small house near her, so I wouldn't be such a burden. Clara is 74, and I just turned 73.

We had such fun playing together when we were kids. We saw each other every Thanksgiving, Christmas and several times during the summer when we came to visit our grandmother out in the country in Mississippi.

You don't forget a bond so close. Even though we don't live near each other now, we have stayed in touch. We write each other at least every other week and even splurge on a long-distance call once a month—always on Saturday nights when the rates are the cheapest.

Clara was married, but her husband died five years ago. She has two grown daughters who live near her. By the way, I was married, too, a long time ago. But not for long. Jack Lewis Martin and I had our ups and downs—mostly downs. He finally left me when I was 45. Left me with nothing. Left me with the memories of three babies that never made it to full term. Paulette is the closest thing to a daughter I've ever had.

Just thinking about it, I'm talking myself into packing up and leaving right now.

## Chapter 15—*Asa*

I haven't run into that pretty girl, Beth Ann Walker, since the first time I saw her in the diner. I could have just imagined her.

I'm supposed to go with John Willard to the store tonight to hear a local band. What else is there to do in this small community? I'd like to head to Memphis one weekend and go hear some real live music at the Mid-South Coliseum. I heard it is quite an adventure. I was thinking about calling Paulette to see if she wants to go over to a little place in the next county to hear some music. I haven't seen much of her lately, either.

When I called her, she sounded different somehow—kinda sad and dull. But I think she was glad to get out with people her age, or so she said. Her daddy gives me the creeps. He's a big, tall, lanky guy who has on khaki pants and a long-sleeved shirt every time I've seen him. He always looks like he needs a shave, and his big work boots are never tied. He is a contrast to her mother, who is at least a foot shorter than he is. She has a sweet smile but looks at her husband for approval every time she speaks. I see sadness in the whole family. I wish Paulette could escape it.

John Willard picked up Milly Sanders, a tall brunette who he dates sometimes. Nothing serious. She is easy to talk to and should be good company for Paulette, who is a little shy. Paulette didn't want us to come to her trailer in the market, but we insisted.

I walked up to the door, dreading the sight of her daddy. Lucky for me, he wasn't home. Her mother greeted us. "So nice of you, Asa, to come out here to get Paulette," she said, brushing a stray strand of hair from her forehead.

I imagined that she must have been a pretty woman in her youth. She is a totally different person when her husband is not around. Smiles come easier, and she looks at you when she is talking to you.

"We were glad to do it. I'll have her back at a decent hour," I said, smiling my "Awe Shucks" smile and backing down the wooden steps. Paulette came out, and we were off.

The band was playing in an old vacant school auditorium. Where the seats had been, there was now a dance floor.

Paulette didn't say much on the ride to the auditorium.  She smiled and responded when I asked her questions or tried to make conversation, but she wasn't as talkative as she was when I saw her last.

We pulled up in the GTO to see a parking lot nearly full. There was every kind of vehicle there from sports cars, to beat-up sedans, to pick-up trucks.

We walked in and the building was mostly dark, except for the sparkling mirror ball hanging in the center of the dance floor. There was a make-shift bar near the front entrance.

Paulette reached for my hand as we walked in. I looked down and gave her a wink. We got some beer and settled at a small round table in the back. It wasn't long before John Willard and Milly were on the dance floor.

After a couple of beers, I finally took

Paulette's hand and led her to the floor—right underneath the ball which was now throwing silver and purple light on the floor. The band was playing a great slow dance song.

It should have been a fun night, but Paulette seemed to be sinking in sadness. As we danced, I felt her trembling in my arms.

"Paulette, what's the matter?  You are shaking."

She didn't say a word but bowed her head into my chest and shook a little more. I tilted her chin up to me, winked at her, and gave her a little kiss. She clung even tighter.

When we got back to the table, I got her a small glass of wine. She was hesitant but finally drank a little and then finished it. The next time we danced, I felt her relax in my arms and take several deep breaths.

And so, the night continued. Every dance felt better, every move was tender, and by the end of the night I felt she had released something dark, but I didn't know exactly what.

On the way home, she sat beside me in the small backseat and rested her head on my shoulder and her hand in mine. She held onto me with an intensity that could only come for a deep need.

## Chapter 16—Paulette

After we went to John Willard's house and got into Asa's farm truck, we started making our way home to the market. It still was about an hour before I knew Daddy would be looking out the window for the headlights to turn into our spot. Right before we made that last turn, Asa said, "Are you sure you are ready to go home?"

"Maybe not yet."

He pulled over to a wooded spot and turned off the ignition. We sat in silence. He cracked the window, and I could feel the dampness and smell the wet leaves. "Do you want to talk about why you are so different tonight? I don't think I've seen a smile since I picked you up."

I burst into tears. He reached over and took me in his arms, smoothing my hair. "You don't have to talk about it. I thought maybe I could help."

"Just hold me. I need to know that all men are not bad."

"What do you mean? Has somebody done something to you?"

I just averted my eyes, looking out my side of the truck window into the darkness. Asa rubbed the back of my neck until I relaxed and turned to face him. His eyes drew me in. The comforting soon turned to much more. I couldn't believe I was letting this happen. It had only been three weeks since the incident with Pete.

This felt so different, so right. No man, or anyone for that matter, had ever touched me with such kindness. I knew this was wrong and only a temporary thing. I also knew that Asa was not in love with me. But that night Asa Sinclair healed a dark spot in my heart.

## Chapter 17—Merry Bell

I've made my decision. I talked to Clara, and we made a plan. I gave notice to the man I rent my space from that I'd be leaving at the end of the month. Clara says she has found me a small two-bedroom, older, house right down the road from her. It's a rental, and that's good so I can see if this move is good for me.

I've got to make decisions about my plants and go through my little shed and make myself throw away those things I thought I'd need but never did. Paulette says she will help me, and her brother Jesse has agreed to put my things in his truck and take me to Tennessee.

Clara lives in a small community in a valley between two mountain ridges in the foothills of the Smokies. That will be new country and a new lifestyle for me.

There is a tourist cabin retreat nearby which offers hiking and horseback trail riding, a grocery store, a little general store, a small-town doctor—about everything I could need. I think I'm actually getting excited.

I told Paulette she could keep the booth open with the existing plants until everything was gone, and I'd split what we made 50/50. She agreed.

I'm worried about Paulette. She just hasn't been herself since her attack. She looks thin and pale and doesn't smile. I wish I could take her with me. She's a senior in high school. If she can just get through this year, there's a chance she can escape this dismal life.

## Chapter 18—Paulette

I sure do miss Merry Bell. She is always so bright and happy. You can't be around her without your spirit lifting. My spirit hasn't lifted in two months. I can't quit crying. It hits at strange moments.

Mrs. Honeycutt, the English teacher and guidance counselor at school, pulled me aside last week and asked what was wrong with me. English is my favorite subject, and she is my favorite teacher.

I felt tears welling in my eyes but choked them back. "If you need to talk, I'm here, okay Paulette?" she said with concern in her eyes.

I think I can trust her. No word from Pete. Also, no news of finding him dead. I was afraid to think of what Jesse had done to him that night. I hope he just scared him away and he went far away from here. His daddy and those sad animals suddenly disappeared from the back of the market camp about that time.

If my sadness doesn't lift, it's good to know that I could talk to Mrs. Honeycutt. Sloan Honeycutt is in her 40s and is beautiful. She is a tiny woman. I'm about five inches taller than she is. Her dark hair is shot with silver with a beautiful silver streak that runs from the part in her hair down past her chin.

She always writes encouraging notations in the margins of my papers along with a few corrections. Now I'm working on an essay competition in hopes of getting a scholarship for college. Well, I'm not really working on it on paper, but running a few thoughts around in my head. Mrs. Honeycutt has taken some of the sections of something I've written and shown me how to make ordinary situations seem extraordinary. For me, that's kinda hard.

After school I go to Merry Bell's old booth and work on the plants. We still have a few customers from town that drive out to get plants for potting or for table decorations. I'm keeping up with the money in a little ledger.

Daddy is working so much these days that I hardly see him. That's a good thing. Mama stays busy scouting for books and other odds and ends and running her booth on market weekends. Jesse has gone to Memphis to do some construction work. He's living with a distant cousin of ours. I hate to think where they might be living. Two guys with no money can't be renting a nice place in a good part of town.

It's been two months since my night with Asa. I think about it all the time. It's easy to imagine that it meant something to him. I've seen him a couple of times, and he greeted me in his usual friendly way. I could tell there was no real spark, so I didn't push things.

I still don't feel right. I think the kind of trauma I went through with Pete has had a physical effect on my body. I cry at the least little thing—happy or sad.

I can't get my appetite back and am losing weight. Mama said something yesterday about my not looking good.  So did Mrs. Honeycutt at school.

My complexion is so fair that you can see prominent blue veins in my temple, especially when I get cold. If I don't feel better next week, I'll go talk to Mrs. Honeycutt.

## Chapter 19—Asa

I'm checking cows this morning horseback. If they are in the front pasture, I can drive around in the truck and check them, but in early spring we have them by the creek. It's a little too rough and muddy in spots to drive.

I threw the blanket and saddle on our old dun horse, looped the strap of the canteen over the saddle horn and checked my gear bag—a rope, antiseptic, old rags, antibiotics and other odds and ends in case I find something hurt or in trouble. I had my fencing tools in another saddle bag.

This day was balmy—damp and cool for early April. I pulled my jean jacket collar up around my ears and headed out. I had plenty to think about.

Last night I finally had a date with Beth Ann Walker. She seems to be coming to see her friend on weekends more often.

We went to a movie in our small-town theatre, ate popcorn, got to know each other a little, and drove around a while before I took her home.

She had been a bit nervous at first, finding it hard to make conversation. By the end of the night, she was chattering like a little bird. Her green eyes sparkled when she talked about her music. She plays the cello in a small community orchestra.

I don't know if she will fit in with my lifestyle. She seems so elegant and refined. What will she see in a cow man like me? It turned out to be a good night with lots of promise.

I feel so guilty about Paulette. Although I do have feelings for her, I never encouraged her to think we might have a real relationship. We shouldn't have let things go as far as they did. I never intended to hurt her.

She seems to be hurting on so many levels. I hoped by spending some time with her, I could bring her out of her sadness. I think I made it worse.

Guess that's enough thinking. You do a lot of that when you are out alone, just you and your horse. In the distance I saw a section of fence that needed checking.

Good thing I was out with my tools. A limb had fallen across the fence, taking that section right down to the ground. I got off and tied my horse to a young tree with the lead rope that I had clipped on the back of the saddle.

"Never tie your horse with reins and a bit in his mouth," I could hear my Daddy warning me over the years. "If he spooks and pulls back, he could cut his tongue."

I'm glad Daddy is still here to give me advice, but he talks to me in my head all the time too.

Thoughts of Paulette and Beth Ann faded as I got out my fencing tools and got to work fixing the downed section. Good thing this was just a cross fence and not a border fence. Can't have cows out on the highway.

As the morning sun moved up in the sky, the early spring day was warming up by the minute.

## Chapter 20—Paulette

By the time I crossed the Tennessee state line, I could tell I was getting sleepy. It was still early morning, and I had several hours to drive to get to Merry Bell's house up around Knoxville. I turned the radio on and opened the window, letting the cool air wake me up.

Jesse had found me a little used Datsun car. It wasn't much. He bought it for me, and I know he really didn't have the money to do that. I plan to pay him back when I can.

I finally got to Merry Bell's little house, it was late afternoon. Her place was just as I had imagined. A small shotgun house set back from the gravel road. The porch was inviting with Merry Bell's beautiful but simple flowers and an old quilt in red and brown colors thrown over the back of a rocking chair. There was a note on the seat of the chair.

Paulette,

I have gone to town to get some groceries. Just make yourself at home. I told you my house was small. Your spot is on the enclosed porch at the back of the house. I should be back soon.

MBM

Every step I took on the porch made the old boards squeak as if walking on them hurt. I placed my few things on the floor in the porch/bedroom, and I fell across the small day bed to catch my breath.

Looking out the bedroom window, I could tell we were in the valley in the foothills of the Smoky Mountains. Trees had not started putting on little green leaves that would forecast the arrival of spring.

My face was hot, and my legs ached. Before I knew it, I was asleep. When I woke up, I was confused. It was almost dark. The orange sun was sitting low in the Western sky and beginning to dip below the mountain tops. I could barely see in the room.

As suddenly as I had fallen asleep, I woke with the full knowledge that being here with Merry Bell was the right place for me and this baby I was carrying.

I'd hadn't gone to the doctor, but I knew. My breasts were tender, I was hungry but sick at my stomach at the same time. Escaping here to Tennessee had been my only option. Daddy was probably still cussing and pitching a fit back home. I'm sure Mama was right in the middle like she always was.

When I told Mama, she cried but hugged me hard. "You better find someplace to go, Paulette, before I have to tell your Daddy. She had given me $100 from her booth money. I knew how hard it had been for her to make that money. I'd have to spend it wisely.

My next step was to find some kind of job. It didn't matter what.

I heard the door open and ran to greet Merry Bell. "Lord girl look at you! Your cheeks are glowing, and your hair is a mess."

I'm sure it was. We laughed and hugged.

We talked non-stop while we put away the groceries, some fun talk and some serious. Her little kitchen was made for only one person, and we kept bumping into each other. It had a smaller-than usual stove and a white porcelain farm sink with a red gingham curtain covering the shelves beneath it.

She introduced me to a tiny, long-haired, black and white kitten with beautiful blue eyes. "That's Maybelline, Maybell for short. Named for my long-lost mare. I always wanted to have a pet in the house but didn't think it would work well at the market."

When we were through in the kitchen, Merry Bell plopped in her favorite chair and put her feet up on a soft stool. Maybell jumped up on the stool and settled between her feet.

"I don't know about Maybell for a name," I said turning up my nose. "That sounds like an old lady cat name," I said, laughing and covering my mouth with my hand.

"Are you calling me an old lady, Miss Priss?" said Merry Bell in a teasing way. "Well, what do you suggest I name her?"

"I think her name is Diana Ross."

"Well, so it is. I just love the Supremes.

See, she's good company for me," said Merry Bell as she stroked the kitten's fur. "I found her down the road at the little store. I think someone had dropped her off. How can people be so mean?"

"I don't know," I said, looking down when I spoke. "Ask Pete's creepy daddy. He would scoop her up, put her in a cage, and sell her if she didn't starve first."

We sat in silence for a while.

## Chapter 21—Asa

We are getting ready to check the spring calves on the place. Daddy and I saddle up, him on the dun and me on the sorrel. It's that kind of day in Mississippi where you can see your breath in the morning and have your bandana up around your ears to cut the wind. By afternoon, you have shucked your jacket and tied it by the long leather strings to the back of your saddle. Before long you'll be rolling up your sleeves.

But right now, it's still cool. The dew is heavy and feels frosted in places. Cows are easy to track on that kind of ground. Daddy goes right, and I go left at a slow pace around the cattle, slowly circling them until they are bunched up in a circle.

I try to hold the herd with a little help from our Border Collie, well-named Drover. He does the Border Collie crouch and stare and holds the cows on his side. Daddy rides slowly into them, checking for any signs of injury or disease for mama cows and babies.

Daddy gets the little silver cow counter out of his jacket pocket and clicks off the number of cows as he circles them to make sure they are all there.

Pretty soon it will be time for spring vaccinations. When we ride among the cows, they get used to us, making a medical round-up much easier. My horse holds still, one ear watching the cattle, the other on me for a cue.

When Daddy has seen enough, he nods, and we slowly open up a hole and wait while the cattle come by at their own pace.

"Nice and slow, Asa," he says. "Don't get in a hurry."

We walk slowly back to the farm side by side, Daddy and me.  He's not a big talker, but he finally breaks the silence.

"Asa, do you think you are going to be happy working with me on this farm and maybe running it one day?" he asked, pushing his hat back on his head so he can get a better look at my face when I answer.

"I think so, Daddy. I'd like to see us try some new things down the road with feeding, grazing, maybe introduce a few new cows to the herd to cross with our line, but for now, I'd say I'm pretty happy."

"I don't want you to feel stuck here. After work you need to go be with your friends your age."

"I do," I say. "There's even this girl I've been seeing—Beth Ann Walker. I'm about ready to bring her out to meet y'all."

"What about that girl Paulette? Is it over with her?"

"It really never got started. Paulette is a good girl who has lived with unfortunate circumstances. She's smart and creative, but there is always a cloud of sadness about her. I never intended for things to get serious between us. I just wanted to be her friend, because I can't tell that she has any."

I watch him for a reaction. Hard to tell if what I said pleases him or not. "I hope I didn't mislead her into thinking it was more than friendship.

He nods, setting back into a slower walk with his horse, hand on his hip, slightly slouched, hat tipped slightly to the right. These are good days. We walk on home. Enough said.

## Chapter 22—Paulette

Even though Merry Bell was retired, she kept busy, and she didn't let my being there change her schedule. She got up every morning, dressed, made a small breakfast and went to one of her "volunteer jobs."  Today was her day to go with Clara to visit residents of a small retirement home.

They visited the 25 residents to see what would make them happy. They each took a wing of the retirement home and found time to sit and talk with each one of the residents.

Sometimes it was a book or magazine that she pulled from her collection of old issues. One lady was proud of her long hair, which, she said, had never been cut. It was hovering about three inches above her knees. Merry Bell would brush it out and braid it every time she went. She depended on the aids to give it a weekly shampoo.

Merry Bell helped a gentleman who had lost most of his vision to write letters to his daughter who lived in Kentucky.

"Oh, those little things don't cost me a penny, and it seems to make a big difference for them to have someone spend some time with them or help them with a task," Merry Bell said as she got ready one morning. "My visits are good for them and good for me, too."

One day a week, Merry Bell worked for a local flower shop booth which was located inside a general store. There was nothing fancy about the booth, just some nice table arrangements, a few corsages around prom time—simple things that didn't require the owner to stock a large inventory.

On Fridays she volunteered at her little mountain church. She made a simple floral arrangement for the Sunday morning service and tidied up around the restrooms and the small space used for a kitchen.

On her day off, she stayed home and puttered in her own flowers and did chores around the house and small yard.

"Paulette," she said suddenly, causing me to jump. She must have been reading my mind. "Get dressed and let's see if we can find you a little something to do. You are going to have to have some money when that baby gets here."

I dressed quickly and did what I could with my hair. We climbed in my old car and off we went, down the mountain to town. By the end of the afternoon we had visited the local hardware store, Marty's Place—a rustic restaurant overlooking the river, and a service station that also sold bait.

Stops at the feed store, the veterinarian, and a place that rented horses for trail rides all yielded no results. Since I was pregnant, I couldn't lift, pick up large dogs at the vet or ride. I was exhausted and a little discouraged.

The next morning was Saturday, so Merry Bell didn't have to be anywhere particular. About 9 the phone rang, and I listened to her side of the conversation.

"Hello. Oh, hi Virginia," Merry Bell said in

her cherry voice.

"Well, yes, she does. We didn't have much luck, no.

"Really?"

"I sure will tell her. That might be perfect. Thanks so much for letting us know." She fumbled for a pen and paper and wrote down something, but I couldn't tell what. I couldn't imagine what this Virginia person was passing along to me.

"Oh, she seems to be settling down just fine. Thanks so much for calling, Virginia. I'll be sure to tell her."

When Merry Bell hung up the phone, she turned and looked at me. She looked pleased as punch.

"What, Merry Bell? What?"

"Virginia is a new friend of mine. Word does travel fast in a small community. Someone at the feed store told her that a young woman was living with me and that we had come in today to inquire about a job." Her blue eyes were just twinkling.

"Virginia was at the library returning some books. The librarian told her they were looking for someone full-time."  She ran over and kissed me on the cheek. "Why, Paulette, if anyone knows books, it's you."

"I haven't gone to college," I said with hesitation. "Will I be qualified?"

"She gave me the number of the librarian. Why don't you call tomorrow and make an appointment with her? You can find out more about the job and ask questions."

I finally began to smile. It did look like God was opening some doors for me. Books had been my salvation once again.

And it was that night that I started reading to my baby.

## Chapter 23—Merry Bell

I am so happy that Paulette is here with me. Oh, my goodness, I feel complete. Never having children of my own, I feel like I have a daughter with a new grandchild on the way. Even if bad circumstances brought Paulette here, I think she is a blessing.

I'm so excited I can hardly calm down enough to sleep. Most nights lately I've been worrying about Paulette. Could she find work, would she be followed by creepy Pete or had Asa broken her heart?

I have almost no money. When I decided to leave Crossroad Market, I sold my little camper and gardening tools to the people who took my spot. That gave me a little money, which I put in the bank up here.

My Social Security check is not much because many of my working years I operated on a cash basis and didn't pay into the system. Luckily, I could claim based on my ex-husband's earnings. At least he was good for something.

Thank goodness the new Medicare government insurance for people over 65 went into effect a few years back. I just couldn't go to the doctor or get my medicine if it weren't for that.

Between Paulette and me, we can make it. I want her to tell the baby's daddy about her pregnancy, but she refuses to talk about it. She's being so independent. I wish she had a good family to support her. If Mr. Toliver would let his wife help her, she would. I think her mama sends her a little of her booth money every couple of weeks but doesn't tell her husband.

But back to our living situation.  I think when the baby comes, I'll move Paulette and the baby into my small bedroom. I can do fine on the porch. I've always loved the view from that window. And if need be, I'll cut out some of that volunteer time and turn it into work time. If I'm able to volunteer, I'm able to work.

While I'm lying here doing all this powerful thinking, I feel a thud right in the middle of my bed. It is only Diana Ross. She has pounced on the bed as if to say it's time to go to sleep. After she sniffs around and purrs, she finds her spot between my feet and curls up in a ball—an instant foot warmer.

How can something so small bring so much love and comfort? She is a happy little kitten even if she is a little spunky at times. Mercy, I haven't even thought how she will be with a baby in the house. I think I'll worry about that a few minutes before I can go to sleep. And lying there in the dark, I heard a small, beautiful voice coming from the porch.

*"Once upon a time there were four little Rabbits, and their names were—Flopsy, Mopsy, Cottontail and Peter..."*

The musical quality of her voice as she continued reading from the works of Beatrix Potter lulled me to sleep.

## Chapter 24—Paulette

Sleep was avoiding me that night. The sounds of Tennessee were similar to those I had left in Mississippi. Seems like where Merry Bell lives, we hear more fox and coyote, their lonesome howls and screams bouncing off the rocks and echoing through the valley.

It was eerie and beautiful at the same time. While I listened to the night music, I said my prayers and then shifted into worry mode. I know the Bible tells us not to worry, and I try not to. I guess I should just call it wonder and concern instead of worry.

I wondered if Pete were alive and if he was, where was he living. He might pop up unannounced at any time.

The last time I talked to Jesse, I questioned him again on Pete's condition. He refused to answer my questions. If he knew how much I worry about whether Pete is alive or dead, he would tell me. I wouldn't pass judgement whatever the situation was.

Supposing Pete is alive, possibly hurt or disfigured, I knew he would have a motive for revenge—for me and especially for Jesse. My brother is a good man. He was only protecting me. And now he has this haunting deed, whatever it was, to carry around with him daily.

If the baby was Pete's, could I love it? If it was Asa's, would I want to find him and tell him?

I didn't have insurance. Merry Bell says I should go to the health department and let them check me out and give me some prenatal vitamins. I can do that tomorrow when I'm in town.

But then I let my mind wander to the job awaiting me. Would I be qualified? Where would I get clothes nice enough to wear to work?

After all that thinking, and worrying, and

making plans, I was finally a little sleepy. I pulled the old quilt up to my chin, turned where I could watch the full moon over the mountains and drifted off into half sleep. Then it was morning.

As soon as I opened my eyes, I got excited just thinking about the job prospect. I called the library and got an appointment to see the head librarian about 9. That hardly gave me time to get ready and drive to town. So, I hit the cold floor of the porch room and got busy.

Finding the only thing I could wear, a blue jumper and white blouse, I brushed my hair and found Merry Bell in the kitchen making herself a cup of coffee and fixing me a glass of juice and some oatmeal. I was so excited that it was hard for me to eat along with the morning queasy spell. Those should be gone soon, so I've read.

"Hey there, sunshine, are you ready for your interview?"

"I guess," I said, eating the last bit of oat-meal I could manage.

"Oh, Honey, you'll do great. You know books, and that will work in your favor. They shouldn't ask about your personal situation, but if they do just tell them you are living with me. I'm a good customer and go to the library all the time."

"Thanks, Merry Bell. I guess I better go so I won't be late." I cranked my little hand-me-down Datsun and noticed that the gas gauge showed that 1 still had a quarter tank. That would be enough to get me to town. I was go-ing to put my $100 in the little bank in town and open an account. I could take out $10 a week for gas and for a little grocery money to add to Merry Bell's pantry.

The library, located on the side street off the town square, was in an old house that sat high off the street. You had to climb a set of steps with wrought iron railings to enter. A friendly lady sat at the front desk and looked up when I opened the leaded-glass doors.

"Hello, young lady, are you Paulette?" yes ma'am.

"Mr. Greer will see you now. First door to

the left down that hall."

*Mr.* Greer, nobody told me that the librarian was a man. I felt my knees weaken. It was okay that he was a man, but I hadn't planned on his being a man. Oh, dear, I turned back to the lady at the desk.

"Could I find the restroom and maybe have a cup of water before I go back?" I asked weakly, trying not to look like my knees were about to buckle.

"Oh, sure. The little kitchen is to your right, and you'll see the restroom back there, too."

I walked down the long, dark wood hall, stepping lightly on the vintage Oriental rug. After I regained my composure, I went back to Mr. Greer's office and knocked. I was sure I'd be met by a pale, old man with glasses down on the end of his nose.

The door opened and a young man, not much older that I was, welcomed me into his office. "Miss Toliver?"

"Yes. I'm here about the library clerk position."

"Come right in. I'm Winston Greer. Did you bring a resume?"

"Well, no. But I can tell you about my

experience."

"Okay. Have a seat and relax."

Mr. Greer was a tall man, so tall that he stooped slightly even at his young age. He had dark brown hair, which was worn a little long, and unique light brown eyes. He didn't look like any librarian I'd ever seen.

"Well, tell me what you know about books."

"My parents and I had a booth at Crossroads Market in North Mississippi and before that at other locations across the South. We specialize in books. Not paperbacks, but classics, legal books, and current titles. We do have paperbacks in the 10¢ box. I had a lady who would let me come and buy bestseller hardbacks when she was through with them."

"What did you do with the books in your booth?' he asked, smiling slightly. I guess I didn't sound too sophisticated.

"I divided them into categories—fiction, classics, non-fiction, and leather-bound books that came from lawyers' offices. We had decorators and book collectors come to our booth on a regular basis to see what we might have."

"I'm impressed, Miss Toliver. Anything else I should know?"

"I've heard that reading to an unborn child has an effect on learning. I've been reading to my baby. I guess it's too early in the interview process to tell you that, but I think you should know. If I get this job, I should be able to work another five months and then return after the baby is born."

"Impressed again. I'm glad you told me about the baby. I'm going to give you a little matching test—books and authors, and you match them up. You can't fail. I just want to see what level reader you might be."

I tried to look unconcerned, and I really was. I'd been looking for book titles and authors since I was 14.

"Okay, Mr. Greer."

He gave me the "test" and sent me to a table in the library to look at it. It didn't take me long to match the books with the authors. I only felt unsure about two out of the twenty on the test. I turned it in to him and waited for a response.

"Thank you, Miss Toliver. I will look this over and my notes from our interview and give you a call. We have to give other candidates a chance to apply until day after tomorrow. Where may I call you?"

I thanked him and gave him Merry Bell's phone number and made my exit. I wobbled down the outside staircase on shaky legs.

As I made my way to the car, I realized I was smiling. I liked this small library, the old house that held it, and the promise of a better life it offered to me. I couldn't wait to hear from him.

## Character 25—Winston Greer

I knew the minute Paulette Toliver walked into my office that I wanted to hire her. She was smart, but uneducated in the formal way. She had scored 100 on the matching author/ book quiz I gave her.

Watching her walk down the path to her car, I wondered what her situation was. I really couldn't ask if she was married, or anything about the baby. I could tell she was trying to make a life for herself and the child. Mrs. Martin was a regular patron, and unusually well-read.

I checked with the receptionist to see if we had any other applicants, but my mind was already made up. It would be hard to wait until day after tomorrow to give her a call and offer her the job.

This was my first time to hire someone. A recent graduate of the University of Tennessee-Knoxville in Library Science, I had taken this job in a small town at a tiny library as a learning experience. My plan was to work here a few months and then go back to college to work on my master's degree.

I was living in a small bedroom on the third floor of the house/library. It was all I needed at this point, but it did make me feel like an old man stuck in the same daily routine. Mainly senior citizens visited the library.

After two days, I called Paulette. "Miss Toliver?" I asked when she answered the phone. "This is Winston Greer at the library. Would you like to come in and talk to me about this position? We would like to offer it to you, but I'll need to go over the terms."

"Oh, yes. Can I come in about 11 this morning?"

I told her that would be fine. "Mrs. Sanders, can you come in here a minute," I said into the phone/intercom system.

Our front desk person, Wendy Sanders,

had the tasks of re-shelving books, answering the phone, providing general information, and assisting patrons. She came quietly into my office, her Mary Jane shoes barely making a sound on the old wide-plank floors.

"Wendy, can you help me make a place for our new clerk to work?"

The house had a grand hall where the reception and check-out desk were located. Stacks had been set up in what was once the parlor and dining room. Antique library tables were in the middle of the both rooms so that patrons could have a place to do research and writing.

The kitchen, though small, served as a break room. My office had been the third and smallest bedroom, and there were two other bedrooms—one used for more stacks, the other was vacant. Some special collections, old bound newspapers, and historical documents were housed upstairs.

"Let's put her in the second room down the hall, the smaller one. It already has some shelves and a desk."

"Have you made up your mind on Miss Toliver?" she asked.

"I think so. Of course, the hiring will have to be approved by the mayor since this is a city library, but I think he will follow my recommendation. Are there tasks that she can help you with to make your job easier?" She thought for a moment.

"I'm talking to her in a few minutes. You can join us before she leaves and get back to me later on what you need her to do."

The front door chimed that someone had come in, and there stood Paulette, all smiles, her face slightly flushed.

"Come in, Miss Toliver. We can go to my office." After we were seated, I began. "I wanted to describe more about this position before we make you a formal offer, which will have to be confirmed by the mayor." She nodded and said nothing.

"The title is for a library clerk, which can mean you can help Wendy with re-shelving materials and assisting patrons who are here to do research. Most of that material is up-stairs. Your hours would be from 3 to 8 p.m. on Mondays. That's the only evening the library is open. The other days are Tuesday through Friday from 10 a.m. to 4 p.m. That's not full-time but enough that we can put you on our city insurance plan. Do you have any questions or suggestions?"

Paulette thought a minute, and finally spoke. "Mr. Greer, I'd be pleased to accept your offer. I do have a few questions, but I have some suggestions too."

I nodded for her to continue. "I love this old house. It's so rich and elegant, but it does look like old people. Would you mind if I brighten up the displays? We could feature some local artist every month? I'd also like to start some children's programs and summer reading camp."

I was impressed again. She was right. It did look like old people in here. The house had a light hint of mold odor which could be devastating if it got into the books. This young woman was smart and creative, even if she hadn't gone to college.

"When would you like to start?"

"Oh, what about tomorrow?" she asked with a slight giggle. "I can start tomorrow. Do you mind my asking about pay and benefits?"

"Absolutely not. We should have gone over all that before now." So as the afternoon wore on, we talked about pay, sick days, vacation days, and insurance.

"Come on, let's go introduce you to Wendy."

"Like Wendy Darling in *Peter Pan*?" she teased.

"Yes, just like in *Peter Pan*."

The old house looked brighter just by her being in it.

## *Chapter 26—Merry Bell*

I couldn't wait for Paulette to get home and tell me how her job interview went. When she did get home, she talked so much and so fast that it was hard to keep up. She was simply bubbling as she told me all about the house, which I had seen, and Mr. Greer and Wendy, about taking the test, and her suggestions for improvement. She finally stopped, fanning her face so that she could catch her breath.

"You better slow down there, girl," I said, smiling at her happiness. "You go freshen up and comb your hair, and we will go somewhere to eat to celebrate your new job."

I think she was glad to have a quiet moment. I could hear her humming to the baby as she got ready. We settled on a nice little Italian restaurant about half way between my house and town. What could be better? I had a a friend who I loved like a daughter and a soon to be grandchild to share my life with. Paulette was away from her abusive daddy and that creepy Pete, and I hoped she was forgetting about Asa. She had a million good things to think about.

We drove to the restaurant and quickly were seated at a round table with red and white checked tablecloths. We ordered, got our drinks and were pouring over the menu. Something caught my eye, just a glimpse of a man in the booth back in the corner.

There was something about the man's gestures and his statue that looked familiar, but I didn't recognize him. I noticed a deep scar that ran from the corner of his eye and down his cheek. The eye, itself, had begun to turn white. Where had I seen him? Probably here in Tennessee somewhere.

We ordered, ate while Paulette chattered some more, and headed back up the mountain to our little house. The day, great as it was, had taken a toll. I heard her reading in the little porch room.

> *"When the first baby laughed for the first time, its laugh broke into a thousand pieces, and they all went skipping about, and that was the beginning of fairies."*
>
> —J.M. Barrie, *Peter Pan*

I climbed into my bed, adjusting the covers while Diana Ross made her nest at my feet. Sleep had almost found me.

I suddenly sat up with a bolt, my heart beating way too fast, my breathing irregular and shallow. Was I having a heart attack? Is this what it feels like? I tried some deep breathing and then it hit me. The man in the restaurant was Pete Lawrence.

## Chapter 27—Asa

I was beginning to feel like I was doing the same thing day in and day out, except when I got to spend some time with Beth. I planned to ask her to join our family for Easter lunch. It was almost time for me to ask her how she felt about getting married. She knows how I feel about her.

She may still plan to work after we get married. We've got plenty of time to talk about all that. Now she teaches music at a private school in Tennessee. It would be nice if she could start a community orchestra here. Guess I'm jumping the gun a little. I haven't even asked.

"Asa! Get a move on, boy," I heard Daddy shout as he entered the shop.

"What are we doing today, Daddy?" I asked.

"Well we have some mechanic work to do on this old Ford tractor. One thing about tractors, they are always broken," He smiled and winked. My dad has a contagious happy spirit about him. It's hard to be around him without your mood lifting.

Mama, on the other hand, could be sweet, but she could get her feathers ruffled like an old, wet hen sometimes. Daddy could tell what kind of mood she was in when she woke up, and he knew which battles were worth fighting.

"When we get through with the tractor, we need to do some repairs on the old catch pen. Won't be long 'til time for spring roundup. Don't you have a buddy who knows something about cattle that could help us that day?" he asked. "If you get somebody in there that doesn't know cattle, they can mess up the whole operation."

"I'll think about it. I think I know a couple," I said. Most of the guys I knew wouldn't take helping with the cows seriously. They didn't realize the money at stake if a cow or calf got hurt or so spooked that it would be hard to handle from then on.

"I'll try to think of someone," I said pulling up an old shop stool and started working on the tractor.

"Dad?" I asked, not wanting to interrupt him when he got too far into the job.

"Yep," he said, never looking up.

"I thought maybe I'd ask Beth to come eat with us Easter weekend. Do you think Mama would mind?"

"You better ask her, son. You know how she is, but I can't imagine she would object. Any special occasion?"

"I want to ask her to marry me but haven't done it yet. I'll let y'all know before long. She is supposed to be here this weekend."

He just winked again and kept working.

Beth drove down for the weekend, staying at her best friend's house, where we met that Friday night. I went to the door and knocked. Most guys these days would have just sat in the truck and honked the horn. My mama would skin me alive if she heard I'd done that.

She and Sarah both greeted me at the door. "What are we going to do tonight, Asa?"

I was thrown off guard, not expecting Sarah to come with us.

"We could meet at the diner. If you let me come in, I'll call John Willard and see if he can meet us there."

"Oh, that would be great. They looked at each other and giggled like girls do when they are together."

The plan worked, and we pulled up at the diner about the time John Willard glided in with the GTO. All three of us were sitting on the bench seat of my work truck. It might have bothered some guys, but not me.

Sarah and John Willard seemed to hit it off right away, so Beth and I did have some one-on-one time. After we ate, we walked downtown, and around the square.

"When are you going home?" I asked,

reaching for her hand.

"Tomorrow, maybe late afternoon," she said, looking up at me. With the streetlight rays backlighting her, I thought at that moment, you better ask her or someone else will.

"Why don't you come to the farm and eat lunch with us tomorrow after church? I can get you back to your Aunt's by 4. That should give you plenty of time to get home."

She thought a minute. "I hate not to spend any time with them. Why don't I eat lunch with them and then come to the farm? You can take me horseback riding like you are always promising."

"Hey, great idea. I think I even have some boots and jeans in the car that belong to Shelly, my sister. You will like her. She's younger than I am and prettier."

"I don't believe that," I teased. "But I will look forward to meeting her and the rest of your family."

We walked another loop around the square and back to the diner to meet John Willard and Sarah. It was not quite the night I'd hoped for, but it had been a good one anyway.

As promised, Beth came out to the farm that Sunday afternoon for a visit and a ride. It was sunny and warm in the late spring. I already had gotten the horses up from the pasture, brushed them, and they were standing, saddled, in the barn lot.

"Have you ridden before?" I asked Beth, watching as she stroked the faces of both horses.

"Maybe a time or two. Put me on a good one."

I put her on the dun. We've always had a dun horse on the place. Daddy just likes them. They don't always come from the same line. This one is a gelding, so I guess I'll have to buy one out of the same line to replace him.

"What color is he, Asa?"

"He's a dun. They can be gray or tan or sandy yellow. Duns always have a stripe down the middle of their backs. See?" I ran my hand down the stripe that came from under the saddle and ended at his tail. "This old guy has been around, and he will take care of you."

"What's his name?"

"Dun. They all get named Dun."

After I helped her up into the saddle and showed her how to hold the reins, we walked around in circles for a few minutes to get the feel of being on the horse.

"Think you're ready?" I ask. She gave me a smile that said she was. We walked away from the barn down into a little meadow. Talk came easy, a good sign in a relationship, I think.

I was glad to see how naturally she sat on the horse, showing no nervousness at all.

"How do you like the place?" I asked, hoping she would like the country life.

"Oh, Asa, I love it. It's beautiful, and I'm sure full of family history. You'll have to tell me more about it."

"Well there is something I want you to see." We rode about another 20 minutes and turned up a hill onto an old trail. I've never known who cut or cleared it. It's just always been there. Just to the right was an old American Beech tree. It towered over all the other trees in the area.

"Can you get down?" I asked.

"Sure, you might have to help me."

But I didn't. She swung her leg over the saddle and dismounted, landing on both feet.

"Just like a pro!"

"Oh, I don't know about that. Why are we down?" she asked, squinting up at me.

I tied the horses to a couple of trees and took her hand, leading her to the beech tree.

"Take a look.  What do you see?"

She looked the tree up and down as she walked around its base. "There are initials on it, Asa! What does that mean?"

"It's our family's carving tree. Our family has been writing on this tree for generations. Notice how some are stretching and fading? The tree grows around, and the initials don't go up any higher than they were when they were carved. Look, here are my mama and daddy's initials, beginning to fade."

She traced the rough marks, taking it all in.

"Do you know all these people?"

"Let's see. Besides mama and daddy, here is my first cousin. He and I are the same age. We used to go camping and squirrel hunting in these woods. One night when we camped out—scariest night of my life with all the night noises. It was country dark except for our little fire and our flashlights which were running low on battery.

"We pretended we were hiding from bad guys. But the next morning before we went in we carved our initials on the tree. See AVS and MLS. No heart or anything romantic around those initials. We must have been about 12."

She smiled and seemed to enjoy all the story telling. "Over here," I took her hand and led her around to the other side of the tree, "is Daddy's brother, my Uncle Earl and his wife. And here….." I turned and looked at her. She was standing with her arms crossed, smiling at me.

"I think it's safe to say that you love this place, this land."

"Sure do. But not as much as I love you. I brought you here to see if you wanted to carve our initials on the tree."

"What will that mean?" she asked, nestling her head into my shoulder and then looking up for my answer.

"It means that I want you to be part of my

life and of this land. I don't have a ring or anything right now. What do you think? Will you
be my bride?"

After a long kiss, she said, "Give me your
pocket knife!"

"Is that a yes?"

"You bet!"

## *Chapter 28—Merry Bell*

When Paulette left this morning for her first day of work, she was just beaming. She had never had a real job where she worked for someone besides helping out in the market. She had fussed and worried about what to wear for an hour last night. It was not like she had much choice. Maternity clothes would be too big, and her clothes were beginning to be too tight.

I told her to go on today, and I'd meet her in town after work and we would pick up a few things. My money was pretty tight. Over the years I had just barely gotten by and had not been able to save much. I did have a small Social Security check monthly, but that was not nearly enough to support us both.

Since the night I realized the man in the booth had been Pete, I have been sick at my stomach. I'm not telling Paulette. Not yet. I honestly don't think he saw us. If he did, he never made eye contact with me and her back was to him. That means he could have been in this area anyway. Or it could mean that he followed her.

I doubt he knows about the baby. Maybe someone from the market heard about it and word got back to him or his daddy. Whatever the situation, it gives me chills.

Suddenly I remembered that one of the ladies who goes to church with me works for the county sheriff. Rennie Masters is younger than I am, in her late 40s. She is a deputy whose assignment usually involves the schools—county, public, and private.

I need to talk to her and get her input. I really want to warn Paulette, but I don't want her to be afraid every time she goes into town. So, the next day I called.

"Hey Rennie, this is Merry Bell Martin. I need to talk to you about a situation and get your input. Is there a time soon that we could meet?"

"Sure, Miss Merry Bell," said Rennie. "Is this an emergency?"

"No, I don't think so. But I don't want to waste time. You'll understand when we talk."

Rennie was silent for a minute. "Do you want to come by this morning about 10, or should I come out to your place?"

"I need to talk when my friend Paulette is not here. Why don't you drive up here if it's not too much trouble?" I asked. My voice was trembling.

"Okay. See you about 10."

After I hung up, I got a legal pad and made some notes. I included anything I remembered about Pete Lawrence, the timeline since Paulette was attacked, and any other information that might be useful.

While I was thinking and making notes, Diana Ross was weaving in and out of my feet under the table. She was pretending that she was hungry when we both knew she had eaten less than an hour ago. The kitten looked up and seemed to give me a sneaky little smile.

It was a good sight to see Rennie pulling up in the driveway a little later in her little black truck. I had already wondered if I had made a mistake in calling her. One of the neighbors might ask Paulette why one of the Sheriff Department's cars was at our house.

"Come on in, Rennie," I said opening the screen door to welcome her inside. "Thanks for coming on short notice."

"Miss Merry Bell you never ask anyone for help, so just the fact that you called made me take note. What's going on?"

We sat at the kitchen table, and I began my story. I told her a little about Paulette's background, about the attack and the rape, and her relationship with the boy back home. I told her that Paulette didn't have her family's support and how she had found her way here to live with me until the baby was born.

"Rennie, last week we were eating in town and I noticed a man out of the corner of my eye. He looked familiar. He had scars that were not there the last time I saw him. It was

Pete Lawrence. I didn't tell Paulette until I talked to you.

"I don't think he knows about the baby. I need to know if it is coincidental that he has relocated to this area or if he is following Paulette. Would you be interested in doing a little off-the-clock detective work for me?"

"Sure, Merry Bell. Let me ask you a few questions and make some notes, and I'll get back to you in a day or two. In the meantime, if you see him again or notice him following her, call immediately. You know I can't report this to the sheriff since it's only a suspicion at this point."

After we finished our official reason for the visit, we sat at the table and talked awhile. I walked her out to the squad car and watched as she drove down the drive back to the county road. I sighed. The first feeling of comfort I'd had in days finally settled the knot in the pit of my stomach.

## *Chapter 29—Paulette*

It was almost time for the library to close. I had to absorb so much information today that I was mentally exhausted. Mr. Greer and Wendy had been patient with me, but I don't guess I knew how much there would be to learn about this job.

Before I left for the day, I visited the children's classic literature section and checked out a couple of books.

Merry Bell was waiting for me in the old town area.

"How did the first day go?" she asked anxiously.

"Oh, great, but there is so much to learn." I brushed my hair back from my eyes. "Where are we going?"

"We need to get you some clothes. Aren't things getting a little snug?" she asked, looking at my tummy and smiling.

"I guess they are. I probably need to find a doctor, too." Merry Bell nodded. Now that I worked at the library, I had insurance through the city. I hadn't wanted to go to the doctor until after I got a job. The monthly checkups at the Health Department had gotten me through this far.

We walked into a small shop downtown. Looking at the prices, I was afraid we were in the wrong place.

"Now Paulette, I don't have much money, as you know, but I want to get you a couple of things. As you start making your own money, you can buy a piece or two at a time," she said.

"I've got money," I protested.

"I know you do. But you better save that for the doctor's bills and baby expense."

Merry Bell knew the lady who owned the shop. She swooped in and took over after I told her my size and what I needed.

"Honey, you are at that in-between stage. Maternity clothes will just swallow you right now. You need a couple of things that are just loose or a size larger than you usually wear. Then you can wear them later after the baby is born."

That was just one more thing I hadn't thought about. She brought out a loose-fitting shift that I could belt later on and a pair of stretchy navy pants. I tried both on, and Merry Belle approved and made the purchase.

"Well, that was easy enough," Merry Bell said as we walked back to our cars.

"I can't thank you enough for all you do for me," I said with tears filling my eyes. Where did that come from? I was not usually a weepy person. Must be the hormones. Seems I am more emotional all the time.

"Why don't I stop at the grocery store and pick up something for supper since you got me the clothes," I suggested.

"That sounds great," said Merry Bell. "I'll go home and see what kind of vegetable I can find to cook."

I watched her get in the car. She had taught me more over these past few months that I'd learned all my years at home. I did miss my Mama and Jesse, but Merry Bell was so interested in everything—books, animals, plants and flowers.

There were those pesky tears again! I cried all the way to the grocery store and was still sniffing as I picked around for the best deal on ground beef.

After cooking supper and clearing the table, I was really tired. Tomorrow will bring a new experience for me at the library. I couldn't wait to wear my new clothes. The first thing I need to buy with my money is a pair of shoes. Mine are looking pretty shabby. After all, they are used shoes from the market—a little scuffed and the heel is worn down by the pattern of the gait of the person who wore them first. Not mine.

I told Merry Belle goodnight and went to my porch/room for the night. I always like to read before I go to sleep. It keeps my brain from replaying conversations and events from the day. And then I read to the baby.

I reached for my old tattered copy of Anna Sewell's *Black Beauty* written in 1877.

This book, though written many years ago, by a British author, had always been an inspiration to me on how to treat animals, ethically and with love. I put my hand over my growing little tummy and read from the book.

*"I hope you will grow up gentle and good, and never learn bad ways; do your work with a good will, lift your feet up well when you trot, and never bite or kick even in play."*
—Anna Sewell, *Black Beauty*

Those words were to a young colt, but they could just as well have been spoken to my little boy. I didn't realize I'd actually said it in my mind. I just knew the baby was a boy. When I imagined our future, I couldn't dream it any other way.

## Chapter 30—Merry Bell

I had just returned from my volunteer job at the retirement home. Struggling to get the door unlocked while holding a small bag of groceries, a sack of cat food and my purse, I got to the ringing phone just in time.

"Hello," I panted into the receiver and dropped my armload of groceries on the table.

"Miss Merry Bell? Sounds like I got you at a bad time. This is Rennie Masters."

"Oh, no Rennie. I'm glad to hear from you. I was just coming in the house with a pile of stuff. What's up?"

"I have some information I can share with you. Can I run out and talk to you in person?

I don't think it will take long."

"Yes, come on. I've been wondering if you had found anything. I will have caught my breath by the time you get here."

"Okay," she said. "See you in a few minutes."

My heart was already beating fast from struggling up the porch steps and coming in the house with an armload of packages. I couldn't wait to hear what Rennie had to say. Even if it was bad news, I needed to know so we could deal with it. I'd have to tell Paulette.

I put my things away, fed Diana Ross, and put on a pot of water to make a pitcher of iced-tea. It helped to stay busy until Rennie got here, so I sliced some lemons.

When I heard the crunching of gravel in the driveway, signaling Rennie's arrival, I went to the porch and opened the door for her.

"Thanks for seeing me, Merry Bell," said Rennie as she pulled up a kitchen chair. She looked official in her black uniform complete with badge and gun belt. I was used to seeing her in street clothes with her hair down. I put a glass of tea in front of her.

"Thanks. You must have known I was

thirsty. Let's go over this information. If you want to take notes, it's fine. We did a background check on Pete Lawrence. Seems he has used different names including Peter Landers, P.W. Brown, and William P. Brown. He has had some charges against him including cruelty to animals, theft, and under William P. Brown there is a sexual assault charge with an underage female in Mississippi.

"We still aren't sure why he is in this area. Seems he is living with a friend or relative in a trailer park a couple of miles outside of town. Did you say he hasn't contacted you and that you didn't think he knew Paulette was here in town?"

"I can't be sure, but I don't think so," I said, beginning to shake. I could feel my hands trembling as I reached for a spoon to sweeten my glass of tea.

"The sheriff would like to assign a detective to watch him for a day or two. It might be hard since we don't have a complaint at this point, and there are no outstanding warrants."

"So, what do we do?" I asked, feeling frustrated.

"I've found a tag number that matches an

old Chevy Impala that he is driving. It doesn't belong to him. Must be the friend's. I think I can tell some of the other deputies to watch out for this vehicle and just see where he is going in town.

"I have a bad suspicion that he might be involved in a dog fighting operation that we have been watching for some time. He could be just observing with the idea of setting up one back in Mississippi or he might even be supplying dogs. Do you remember if he had any big or vicious dogs back at Crossroads?"

"Oh, goodness. I don't remember. But I tried to avoid his daddy's operation. We all knew it wasn't a legitimate pet booth. I suspected a puppy mill was his supply along with some stolen dogs."

"Merry Bell, just keep your eyes open. I wouldn't tell Paulette at this point. It would only upset her. No proof that he is here to watch her. If he doesn't know about the baby, he has no motive to be looking for her. Even if he did know, he doesn't seem like the type of guy who would want the responsibility of being a single dad caring for a newborn. Give me a call if you see or hear anything, okay?"

"Rennie, he does have a motive. Revenge. It was Paulette's brother Jesse who put that bad scar on his face and left him with a blind eye. His motive is pure revenge."

## Chapter 31—Paulette

Merry Bell has been very quiet lately and a little jumpy. I hope she is not worrying about my being here or about money. I know I make a strain on her budget and her life in general.

I decided to do something to cheer her up.

After doing a little investigating, I found a woman who teaches beginning riding lessons. She left an index card on the bulletin board at the veterinarian's office.

BEGINNER HORSEBACK LESSONS. PRIVATE SESSIONS FOR CHILDREN AND ADULTS. SPECIALIZING IN LESSONS FOR THOSE WITH DISABILITIES. GENTLE HORSES. CALL FOR AN APPOINTMENT. CHARLENE "CHARLEY" ROSS.

I gave her a call.

"Hi, Ms. Charlene, my name is Paulette Toliver. I'd like to get some information about your program."

"Hello there Paulette; please call me Charley. What can I do for you?"

"I have a friend in her early 70s. She was quite a hand with horses in her younger days but hasn't ridden in years. Do you have anything gentle enough that we could put her on and just let her walk around? It would mean so much to her."

"I might have just the horse for that," she said in a cheery voice. "Do you want to come out and take a look for yourself before you bring her?"

"Oh, that would be great. I work at the library. I can come about five this afternoon. Is that okay with you?"

We agreed on the time, and she gave me directions to her place. It was summer, so we had a little daylight left at that time of day. After work I headed out to her place, about 10 minutes outside of town.

Charley came out to meet me when I got out of the car. She was a tall, slender woman who wore her blonde hair shot with gray braided into a long plait down her back. She wore jeans tucked into well-worn boots and an oversize chambray shirt tied at the waist. She has bright blue eyes and skin that showed signs of years of outdoor living.

Her house was a typical one-story 1930 farm house. The barn was older but was kept clean and well-organized. There was a small area with sandy ground, enclosed by cattle panels where she held her lessons.

Charley walked over, taking long strides, and extended her hand. "Nice to meet you, Paulette. Tell me more about your friend."

"I'd just like to surprise her with a little riding session. She thinks she will never ride again. She doesn't have any real disability, just the usual aches and pains for someone her age. She would need help getting on."

"That's no problem. Come on to the barn and I'll introduce you to Rowdy. Don't let the name scare you.  He doesn't have a rowdy bone in his body."

We walked over to the barn which had six stalls along one side and stalls for feed, hay and tack on the other side. Rowdy was standing calmly, munching on his afternoon flake of hay. He was a nice-looking old guy—still in good shape for being about 20 years old.

"He's what you call a flea-bitten gray. That's an almost white or light gray horse with darker flecks in his coat. He always looks a little dirty even when he's not." Rowdy's mane was long, reaching down past his neck. That was a sure sign that he had been groomed on a regular basis.

"He's just a good using horse. I bought him off a ranch about five years ago. When we get riders, who are a little nervous or who have never ridden at all, we put them on Rowdy. He will be fine for your friend, but I will walk along side of her until she feels comfortable."

We agreed on Saturday morning for the session with Merry Bell.

Friday night I told Merry Bell that I wanted her to go with me to look at a used baby bed.

I dressed in the only jeans I could still fit in. Merry Bell must have taken my cue and came out wearing an old pair of slacks. I threw light jackets for both of us in the back seat.

We pulled up at Charley's house. "Oh, look, Merry Bell, I think this lady has horses. Let's go look at them."

She seemed hesitant. "Oh, come on," I said taking her by the hand and leading her to the pen. About that time Charley came out and introduced herself. Merry Bell began to show a little interest in the horses and asked a few questions.

We looked at a little bay mare in a side lot and a big chestnut Quarter Horse nearby. "Come to the barn with me," Charley said to Merry Bell. "I'll show you one of my favorites."

When we got to the barn, Rowdy was saddled and cross-tied in the barn hall. "This is Rowdy," said Charley. "He has a lesson in a few minutes, and by the way, he's anything but rowdy."

"What kind of lesson?" asked Merry Bell. She had begun to stroke the horse's neck.

"Let me check my book," said Charley, pretending to check her appointment book.

"It says here Rowdy is giving a refresher lesson to Merry Bell Martin, who was quite a hand in her day."

Merry Bell stared in disbelief. "What in the world? Paulette, did you have anything to do with this? You know I can't get up on a horse." The whole time she was fussing, a slight smile was creeping across her face.

"Come on Merry Bell," urged Charley. "Let's take him out to the riding pen and see what we can do."

Charley put a bridle on the horse and led him to the pen. First, she rode him, herself so that Merry Bell could see that he was a well-mannered gentleman, calm and relaxed.

"What do you think?" I asked.

My friend took a deep breath, blew it out, and smiled. "Is this why you suggested I wear pants?"

I took that as a yes and nodded to Charley who was holding Rowdy. She led him to the center of the lesson pen.

"How am I going to get up," asked Merry Bell, trembling as she ran her hand down Rowdy's neck and stretched her hand out, palm open, in the horseman's handshake. He inhaled deeply.

"You are just going to get on," said Charley. "Here hold him while I get the mounting stool." Merry Bell reached up and held the lead rope that was attached to the halter underneath the bridle.

Charley brought a well-worn three-step stool over to the horse and placed it very closely underneath the stirrup. "I've already taken the stirrups up to where I think they might fit you, Mrs. Martin."

"Oh, shoot. That sounds like you are talking to my ex-mother-in-law. Just call me Merry Bell. Okay, I'm ready."

Charley held the horse while I steadied Merry Bell as she took one, then two, and finally three steps to the top of the stool. The stirrup was just another step a few inches higher.

Merry Bell grabbed the reins and horn and swung her leg over the back of the saddle just like she did the last time she rode Maybelline. She gathered her reins, adjusted her feet in the stirrups, and smiled down at us.

"By George, I think she's got it after all," said Charley in an affected British accent.

Charley still had the lead rope attached to Rowdy's halter. "Just sit there and get yourself together, and then we are going to walk some circles."

Merry Bell sat up straight, collected her reins at the base of the horse's neck, toes up, heels down…. she took the first step and then another and then walked a perfect circle.

They made several circles to the right, then to the left, and she pulled the horse into the center.

"How does he feel to you, Merry Bell," asked Charley.

"Like I never should have gotten off." With that Charley unsnapped the lead rope and Merry Bell urged the gray horse on with a slight tap of her heel to the rail. They walked more circles, and then Merry Bell clucked, put her heel in the horse's side and moved into a nice little trot. Her hair had come partially down and little wisps were framing her face.

Charley and I looked at each other in amazement. "I'll be damned," Charley said, kicking the dirt with the toe of her boot. "You just never know."

## *Chapter 32—Paulette,*
### *four months later*

Today I'm about too round in the middle to wear anything I have in my closet. By my calculations, I'm about seven and a half months pregnant—give or take a week or two. Besides being clumsy, having swollen feet, and popping the buttons around my mid-section, all is good.

I have quit worrying about this baby. I made the decision to love him or her, no matter who the father is. My heart tells me it is a boy. I've been thinking of boy names. No girl names come to mind. That's another sign that it's a boy. Merry Bell says I will have to wait til I see him to name him. His name needs to fit his personality.

It's September and days are still hot. After work, I prop by fat little feet up on a stool while Merry Bell and I talk and watch TV.

I have always read newspapers. Pretty nerdy my friends say, for someone my age. Merry Bell and I always watch the news at 5 in the evening and at 10 at night—the signal that it's bedtime. That habit intensified not long after I moved here.

Last April we watched TV coverage of the assassination of Dr. Martin Luther King, Jr., civil rights leader, by James Earl Ray. We sat looking at her little TV as the networks covered the race riots and violence that followed.

It happened again June 5, when U.S. Senator Robert Kennedy was assassinated by Sirhan Sirhan following Kennedy's victory speech for winning the California presidential primary. Surely the rest of the year will be peaceful.

Sometimes when I'm reading to my stomach or just sitting with my hand resting on my belly, I catch Merry Bell looking at me with a sweet but sad smile. I can't imagine losing three babies. She told me that she lost the first two early in her pregnancy. The third little one had begun to come alive inside her, kicking its tiny feet, getting the hiccups, and rolling from side to side.

When she went into early labor at six months, it was just too early. The hospital sent Merry Bell and Jack home to bury their baby. She dressed him in a little angel gown made by a women's group who crafted hand-sewn gowns for babies who were stillborn or didn't make it home from the hospital.

They buried him at a small cemetery in the mountains  where most of the graves were as old as Civil War times. The stone fence bordering the grounds was crumbling, and many of the headstones were leaning.

The one time Merry Bell talked to me about this she said, "The graves underneath the century-old cedars are just beautiful, Paulette. Not many people in the area know the cemetery is there. I wanted him to be somewhere that mattered. I thought about those young boys who had fought and died, and I knew that place mattered."

She had gotten permission to bury her baby there from the elders at the little church that sat next to the hallowed ground. A group from the church made sure the cemetery was well-tended. Merry Bell had moved so much, that she knew she would have to leave her baby's grave behind, but the beauty and serenity of that old churchyard gave her a special kind of peace.

I prayed every night for the safe delivery of my baby. The first few months of my pregnancy I was in shock. So much had happened—the attack from Pete, the wonderful but hasty night with Asa, leaving my parents, and moving to Tennessee with Merry Bell.

My job at the library had made the time go fast. I had found a new friend in Wendy, who was about five years older than I am. Winston Greer is like no man I've ever known. He is so interested in everything. He travels, reads constantly, loves art and animals.

At lunch, we usually eat at the little round table in the kitchen and talk about whatever he has been doing. I get the feeling that he is lonesome for some younger friends, too. Here we are, three young people, trapped in the quaint and beautiful mountain town, populated by mostly retirees.

## Chapter 33—Merry Belle

I haven't seen anything of Pete in the last few months. I'd like to think he has left town, but according to Rennie, he has not. He's laying low whatever he is doing.

Paulette is bound to see him sooner or later. That means he will see her and assume she is carrying his child. I wonder what made him zero in on her as a target in the first place. I guess because she was a pretty young girl who was vulnerable, he thought it would be a game to torment her. There could be other girls in other towns who he has victimized. I can't think about this anymore, or I will be a nervous wreck.

It is so fun watching Paulette get ready for

the birth of her baby. Soon I will find someone who can help me move the furniture around so that she can have the bigger bedroom.

I have picked up a few things for the baby—a blanket, some little gowns. But she will need so much. We can go shopping at some thrift shops and see if we can find a good but used baby bed.

I'm happy that Paulette has made friends with Wendy at work. They seem to get along great. Growing up on the road, moving from town to town, Paulette never had a close friend. They work together all day and then talk on the phone most every night.

Wendy is married and has a little girl about a year old. She has been able to give Paulette some advice and will be a good support person for her later. She has me, but I'm sure Wendy will have better advice about dealing with a newborn. I hear they aren't always cooperative.

I think Wendy has introduced Paulette to more of her friends, so she will get to know people her age. They are planning a secret baby shower for her at the library in a few weeks. Things just seem to be falling into place so nicely.

Paulette has been able to save a little money and having insurance through the library has helped. She found a doctor she likes about 30 miles north of here, in a town that has a small hospital.

Every night at supper she talks a blue streak about the library and the displays she set up in the front window and behind the reception desk.

She got permission to go to the local elementary school once a month and do a reading to first and second graders. They all got library cards, and it wasn't long before their parents were bringing them in to get books. The parents even got cards and got books for themselves.

Mr. Greer is very pleased with her efforts. I think he might be a little smitten with her, if you ask me.

I told Paulette that I would give up most of my volunteer work after the baby is born to keep him or her, so that she can keep working. As long as my health holds out, I think that's the best volunteer work I can do.

## Chapter 34—Pete Lawrence

I had quite a surprise this morning as I sat in my car on a side street downtown. I was waiting on my cousin, Rowland Harris. We are up here in this little town to set up a little dog fighting action and other entertainment for one of the richest men in the state. He has a vacation home up here and likes to invite some of his high roller buddies for weekends of action—a little poker, a lot of drinking, bragging, and loud talking.

The street where I've parked is pretty quiet. Nothing much here except the town library. I see Rowland from a distance coming down the street toward me. Rowland is usually involved in activities that are just on the border of being criminal. Some cross the line.

My cousin is tall and skinny. Lucky for him, he just blends in—nothing unusual about him that would make you notice or remember him. He's just your average poor white trash. Row always looks like he is just a little dirty—stubble three days old, scuffed shoes, clothes that look like he just got off working a 12-hour night shift in a factory.

Rowland has been in this part of Tennessee for a couple of years. He found a used trailer to rent. The owner of the trailer lives on a now-inactive farm. He had used the trailer to house seasonal farm workers. So, it's perfect for Row. It sits behind an old cow barn. It's out of sight, nothing that would draw attention.

Then I notice this girl walking down the sidewalk toward the library. She's blonde, young, and there is something familiar about her. I look again. She's pregnant. I can't believe my eyes. It's Paulette Toliver from the Market.

I did mental math. I must have had my little fun with her back in March. I count the months. It's near the end of October. That kid is probably mine. Wow.

I sure don't want to take on raising a kid. I'll see if Rowland can find out what she is doing up here and where she lives. If she is with someone with a little money, I might be able to work a deal.

Looks like she might be ready to have that baby soon. I better get the facts so that I can do some planning.

Rowland scares me a little when he jerks the passenger side door open and hops in the car.

"Hey Row," I say. "See that girl?"

"The pregnant one?"

"Yeah. Her name is Paulette Toliver. See if you can find out something about her. Where she lives, if she works, anything you can find."

"Any reason we are interested in this gal?" he asks wiping his nose on the sleeve of his jacket.

"Not that you need to know right now."

I crank the car, and we are off to meet with our client. The wheels in my brain are spinning out of control.

## Chapter 35—Paulette

Well, it's almost time. Today I told Winston that I needed to go home and begin my maternity leave. I'd hate for something embarrassing to happen at work.

Wendy surprised me with a baby shower at the library. Merry Bell and Clara were there as were some of the friends I've made through the library. I wish my mother could be there. She keeps in touch but hasn't been to see me. I hope she will come when the baby is born.

Clara gave me a quilt that she had pieced and quilted by hand. She had embroidered little ducks, rabbits, foxes, and birds on the squares. The sashing was blue. Wendy gave me a big basket full of everything you could think of that a baby would need—diapers, tiny little nail scissors, nightgowns in several sizes, pacifiers, a thermometer, all things that only someone who has had a baby recently would know that I need. The basket was big enough that I could use it as a bassinette for a few weeks.

The present that made me cry was a set of little books from Winston. Yes, he got to come, too. They were written by a local Tennessee author and illustrated with little ducks, rabbits, foxes, and birds that looked coincidentally like the squares of the quilt. Clara and Winston must have collaborated on those gifts.

Right before the shower ended, Wendy said, "One more present. This came in the mail for you yesterday, Paulette." She handed me a little white box tied with a white ribbon. "Open it!" said Merry Bell.

"Looks like the baby will be well-taken care of. I wanted you to have a present from me at your shower," my mother had written on a little white card. I opened the box. Inside was a small, gold locket. One side for a lock of the baby's hair and one side for a photo of the child. I could feel my lower lip quivering and tears welling in my eyes.

"Stupid pregnancy hormones," I said, choking back the tears. "Let's get some cake."

And we did. Little white petit fours with miniature baby booties in pink and blue on top. Up until today, the whole situation had been surreal. Now that I saw actual clothes and blankets and pacifiers I got a knot in my stomach. Could I do this? I looked over at Merry Bell.  She nodded and smiled as if to say, "Yes, you can."

We all hugged, and the ladies helped me load the presents in my car. While opening the passenger side door, I noticed a little piece of paper on the windshield, under the wiper.

"Oh no," I thought. Surely, I hadn't gotten a ticket.

Balancing the basket with all the presents inside, I snatched the paper off the windshield.

*"Well, if it isn't little Paulette."*

My heart felt like it had stopped in my chest. I almost dropped the basket, and, I literally felt the blood drain from my face.

Looking up, I scanned the street, nearby lawns, looking for parked cars or any sign of Pete Lawrence.

"What's the matter, Paulette?" asked Merry Bell, helping me balance. She took the basket from me, and I handed her the note. As she read it, she had a reaction almost identical to mine.

My perfect day had been ruined.

## *Chapter 36—Paulette*

This night has been the longest ever. I had just gotten to sleep when I felt a little heel right under my ribs, just kicking up a storm. I could feel the baby wiggling and stretching. I think he was getting in position. I sure hope so. As scary as the thought of me with a newborn is, I'm ready to meet this little person.

I don't think I've really slept all night in two weeks, not since I found the note from Pete on the windshield, not since the baby seemed to want to pounce on my bladder all night.

I finally drifted to sleep, and around 3 a.m., woke in a puddle of water. I made my way to the bathroom, changed clothes and went in to wake up Merry Bell.

The contractions were small now, but I didn't want to be on the road with them any stronger. We collected my already-packed bag and headed out to the car.

"Just get in Merry Bell, I'm driving."

"Oh, no, you're not."

"You can't see at night and you know it. If the pains get bad, I'll pull over and let you drive. If we hurry, we will get to the hospital before that happens."

I tried not to panic or Merry Bell would be in worse shape that I was. We had talked about this night, but all plans seemed to have flown a part.

I finally convinced her to let me drive, and away we went. The night sky was clear with a full moon and twinkling stars. I've heard that maternity wards are overflowing when there is a full moon. Looks like, for me, it might be true.

We arrived safely at the hospital, pains coming more regularly now.

"Do I need to call anybody for you?" asked Merry Bell.

"No. Let's just wait for everything to be over."

I filled out the necessary paperwork and a nurse took me back to check my progress.

"Mrs. Toliver, looks like you might have a baby in about three hours or so. Let's get you to a room. My name is Lonnie, and I'll be taking care of you tonight."

I didn't correct her on the Mrs. She put me in a room and hooked me up to a monitor to check the baby's heartbeat and mine too. Merry Bell came in, and we waited.

The contractions began to come hard at regular intervals. They were so bad they took my breath away. Lonnie put a cool towel on my head. She had beautiful hands and nails, I noticed as she pressed the towel to my forehead.

"Are you going to have good help at home?" she asked. "First babies are a lot of work. I hope your husband can be there at home the first few days."

"Miss Lonnie, I'm not married," I confessed in between contractions when I could get enough breath to talk. "I live with Merry Bell Martin, and she and her cousin Clara will be all the help I need."

Just when the pain got so bad I thought

I was being ripped in two, an orderly and Nurse Lonnie wheeled me to the delivery room where I saw my doctor. Boy, was I glad to see him!

After the last really bad pain I felt a mask over my face. The clock read 6 a.m. The lights went out.

"Miss Toliver, honey, wake up.  We have somebody for you to meet," said Lonnie, who looked a little out of focus. She handed me a little blue-blanketed bundle.

Gingerly, I peeled back the blanket and saw a blonde, fuzzy head. I peeled back another layer and looked into the most beautiful light blue eyes I'd ever seen. I took a deep breath, thanked God, and held my baby as tears of relief poured down my cheeks.

## *Part 2*
## *Chapter 37—Merry Bell*

I can't believe how fast these last few years have flown by. Paulette named her baby John Vincent Toliver. He is the most beautiful little three-year-old boy I think I've ever seen. All that reading his mama did to him while he was in her tummy must have paid off. He will sit in my lap and let me read to him as long as I still have a voice.

Paulette is still working at the library and doing well. I think she and Mr. Greer have struck up quite a friendship. She has made new friends, and I'm glad to keep John while she goes to lunch or a movie.

The dark cloud of Pete still hovers over us. When she was still in the hospital, the florist delivered a single red rose to her room.  The card read, "Can't wait to meet the kid."

She knew it was from Pete. We thought of ways we could let him know that the boy was not his child, but nothing seemed in our best interest. If he knew John was another man's child, he would torment her and spread gossip around town just to hurt her. I think he just makes it his hobby to pop up every now and then to scare her.

One night when John was about a year old, I asked her if she had ever considered telling Asa that the baby was his. He's such a good man. I feel sure he would do the right thing.

She wouldn't hear of it. Finally, she said she had gotten a letter from her mama telling her that Asa had gotten married, and they had recently had a baby girl. It just didn't seem to be the right time, she said. "Maybe one day when John is older."

Her mother had stayed in touch. Paulette's daddy died last year. That had allowed her mother to come up here to visit more often, and she called her mama long distance about twice a month.

If you ask me, it's about time Paulette took

the baby and went home, just for a visit mind you. She needs to see her mama and her brother. I need her to come back. Lord, I just can't imagine my life without Paulette and John in it.

## Chapter 38—Paulette

Merry Bell has been after me for years to go home for a visit. I wrote Jesse and asked him if he would meet me there. I want John to spend time with my brother. He needs the influence of a man in his life.

Three days later I got the response I was hoping for. He said he could take off a few days and meet me at mama's. He said he would be coming alone. He and his wife have two little girls under four years old. It might be too overwhelming to mama to have all of us there, he thought.

Since Daddy died, Mama moved out of the trailer at the market and found a small house in town to rent. It's sad. I know how hard they worked all their lives, and now she has so little to show for it.

I packed John in the backseat of the car, and we headed to Mississippi. He was good all the time, and I expected the same on the drive there. I put a bag of his favorite toys next to him on the seat.

We made a couple of stops on the way, just to get out and stretch and visit the restroom. I was always leery about traveling alone. We got back in the car, and I locked the doors. I got out a few snacks that Merry Bell had packed for us.

John munched on his crackers and slices of cheese and then chattered to himself until he went to sleep.

When I pulled up at mama's house, she came running out to meet me. "Oh, he's asleep. I hate to wake him," she said, looking up at me.

"It's okay. He slept a good bit on the trip. Since we are in a strange location, let me wake him up."

I patted his leg and watched him stir. I was always amazed at the beauty of this little boy. How could I be so lucky for him to be mine? I reached in, and he stretched his arms out for me to take him. When he got out of the car, he ran to Mama. Her visits had paid off. He recognized her.

She knelt and opened her arms. With John she was a different person, much warmer and more relaxed.

When Jesse got here he couldn't wait to do a little roughhousing with John. He loved it. I smiled as Jesse's big frame lay on the floor with John climbing all over him. This was what he needed. How could I have not known he was missing so much?

After lunch Jesse and I took a walk while little John was napping with Mama. "So, are you happy up there with Merry Bell? Do you feel safe"

"I'm very happy there," I said looking up into his hazel eyes. "I love my job, and I've made some good friends. For the most part, life is good."

"What's the bad part," he asked, getting right to the point.

"Tell me, Jesse, about the night Pete attacked me. What did you do to him?"

"I hope I took care of him, why?"

"He is staying up there in Tennessee close to where I live, but I'm not exactly sure where. Merry Bell saw him up close once in a restaurant. He had scars on his face and one eye looked like it was blind. Was that your doing?"

"Could be," said Jesse, the veins popping out in his temple. "Has he contacted you?"

"Just enough to keep me scared. He's left notes on my car, and sent a flower and creepy note to the hospital when the baby was born. He thinks the baby is his."

"You've never confronted him?"

"No. Merry Bell has a friend who works for the sheriff's office, and she has done a little on-the-side-detective work. Seems he may have a partner and be in the illegal side of the dog business. She is keeping an eye on him."

"Let me think about all this and see if I can figure out the best move," said Jesse. "You call me, COLLECT, the next time you get a note, a call, see him or anything. You understand?"

I nodded and felt tears coming down my face as I linked arms with my brother.

This morning I decided to go to church before I headed home. That's something that has been missing in my life. Mama and Jesse said they would keep John while I went.

I drove up to the little white church and quietly entered the back door. I found a seat near the back. A few people smiled and nodded, but I doubt they remembered me.

Then my breath caught in my throat. Sitting just a few pews ahead of me was Asa, his arm around his new dark-haired wife who was holding a baby about six months old.

Just the sight of him made me tremble. It always had. He had on a chambray blue shirt, and you could see the imprint of his hatband on his thick light-brown hair.

As we stood up to sing "Amazing Grace," I thought I'd slip out the door. Just then, the baby started crying, and Asa picked her up and headed for the church door. That's when he saw me. Our eyes met.

When the song finished, I, too, went outside to head straight for my car.

"Paulette," he called from behind. He was rushing to catch up with me. The baby had quit fussing and smiled a toothless grin at me that made me laugh and relax.

"Hi Asa, so good to see you, and who is this?"

'This is Lora Madison Sinclair, and she always finds a way to get out of church early." He smiled down at me. "How are you? I've wondered these last few years."

"I'm okay. I live with Merry Bell Martin. Do you remember her from the flower booth at the market? I work at a little library in a small town near Knoxville, Tennessee."

"I do remember her. Good for you," he said, and seemed genuinely pleased.

"And I have a little boy. John Toliver."

"What?!  Where is he? I'd love to meet him. How old is he?"

"Three, almost four."

I could see wheels turning in his head. About that time Beth came up to join us, and he introduced her to me. She was so quiet and pretty, and absolutely lovely. I couldn't blame him for loving her. She took little Lora and bounced her on her hip.

"Beth, I'm going to walk Paulette to her car, and then I'll be right along."

We walked beneath the old cedars that separated the church yard from the old cemetery next door.

"Paulette, I hope I didn't cause you hurt. We were both so young. If you ever want to come back to be close to your mama, I have a little house on the farm that is vacant. You and your little boy would be welcome to stay there."

"Asa, thank you. I love Merry Bell so much. I'd hate to leave her, but if I ever have to, I might take you up on that offer. John will be in kindergarten next year, and I can't get her to keep him and get him back and forth to school..."

"Just let me know. I've gotta get back to Beth and the baby. Really good to see you."

"Same here, Asa." It was all I could do not to reach up and hug him.

## *Chaapter 39—Merry Bell*

While Paulette has been gone, I've been trying to stay busy. Sometimes it's hard. I let some of my volunteer jobs go when John came along so that I could be here with him.

I'm looking out the window as the sunrise paints the distant mountains a rich pink. If I look away for just a minute, the color will have changed, and more blue will emerge. While I'm enjoying the peace and feeling blessed, the breath is suddenly knocked out of me by Diana Ross as she pounces right in the middle of my stomach.

"You are a devil cat," I say as she flips over on her back for me to rub her stomach. By domestic cat standards, she is small. But she doesn't know that. She thinks she is a grand lioness that rules our home.

So, I sit and rub and scratch while she purrs until she finally takes a nap, still upside down.

That peaceful moment was good for my soul since I've been so tense lately. I've seen a car driving past the house with the lights low, just creeping by. I'm pretty sure it's Pete. I just can't imagine why he wants to torment Paulette so. Is he thinking the baby is his? Or is he so evil that he just enjoys making her life miserable?

As Rennie says, "We can't charge him until he does something."

Well, it wasn't long before he did.

Paulette got home about 4 the next afternoon. She was tired but smiling and couldn't wait to tell me about her trip back to visit her mama, and going to church, and seeing Asa and his family.

I think she was genuinely happy for them,

but a little sad at the same time. She brought in her bag and the baby things, but there were still odds and ends in the car to get. On her second trip out, I watched out the window and saw the same beat up car creeping past. It stopped near the drive way, and my heart stopped too.

I listened and watched as brave little Paulette approached the car. She kept her distance. Pete rolled down the window.

"Well, if it isn't little Paulette.  Where's my kid?"

"What do you want?" yelled Paulette, showing no fear but keeping her distance from him and the car.

He just licked his lips and sneered at her. "I want to see my kid."

"Pete, he isn't yours!"

"How do you know that? Were you sleeping around with other guys, too?"

She did not respond.

John was sitting on the floor, playing with some little toy trucks, unaware of the tension that must have flowed from me.

I went in my room, reached in the back of the closet, and found an old revolver wrapped in a bandana handkerchief. I had held on to that gun in case of emergency. It probably hadn't been shot in 20 years. I checked the chamber and tucked it into my apron pocket and returned to my place at the window.

I could tell they were arguing but couldn't make out what they were saying. Then Paulette raised her voice.

"He's not your child, Pete! He has blonde hair and light blue eyes. How could he be?"

Pete sat there in the car for a few seconds as if pondering his next tirade.

"I won't believe you till I see him. Bring him out."

"No," said Paulette emphatically.

"Alright woman have it your way. One day when you come home, he won't be here. That old woman won't be no match for me. You'll see."

Paulette turned her back to him and marched into the house.

"I'll be back," he said and slowly rolled up the window and left, spewing gravel onto her car.

When she came in, she released the fear she had hidden from him. The girl was trembling from head to toe and collapsed and sat with her back leaning against the wall.

"Paulette," I told her. "Now we can call the sheriff's department and report him. He made verbal threats. Help is on the way, Baby."

She drew her legs up and crossed her arms over them and then rested her head there while she sobbed.

"Hi, my name is Merry Bell Martin, I need to file a report....," I spoke into the old black receiver.

## Chapter 40—Pete

You will never convince me that baby is not mine. Who would want to fool around with Paulette, that shy, skittish girl?

If the kid is not mine, then whose? I did see her hanging around with Asa Sinclair a few times. If I play my cards right, this might work out better than my original plan.

I could take the kid and demand ransom from Asa and his old man. The Sinclairs don't live the high life, but they have money. And they have land, which equals money.

The little plan for dog fighting that Rowland and I came up here to check out will look like pocket change compared to the new scam.

Rowland will be in on it. He doesn't come up with ideas, but he's pretty good in carrying them out. Now I have to convince him, and then work out the details.

## Chapter 41—Paulette

I didn't wait for the Sheriff's Department to take action. First, I called my brother and told him what I was planning to do. Next, I called Asa.

The operator gave me the phone number. I waited until I knew he would be in the house after doing farm work, about 7 that night. I dialed, with steady hands, and no tremble in my voice.

"Asa? This is Paulette Toliver."

He hesitated. "Hello Paulette, good to hear from you again."

He must have been wondering if I was going to make some trouble.

"You mentioned when I was visiting last week that you had a tenant house available. Is it still available? I'm having a few issues up here and need to get down there closer to

Mama."

"Well, yes, I do. It's about a mile from the homeplace. And it's not much. Just a little white house with two bedrooms, living room, small kitchen and a bath. I can do a little cleaning before you come if you want it."

"I do. How much is it?"

"Oh, what about $50 a month?"

"Fine. When can I move it? I will be needing it soon."

"Give me a day or two, and you can come by this weekend if you need it that soon."

"Deal.  Oh, will it be okay if I plant a few flowers and grow some vegetables out back? If it is, I may bring Merry Bell with me for a few weeks until my little boy gets settled in."

"Oh, sure."

I thanked him and hung up. I'm sure he wondered what in the world I was up to.

After John went to sleep, I went into Merry Bell's room where she was reading by the small lamp next to her bed.

"Hey Paulette, what's the matter?"

"I have made a decision. I am going to take John and move into a small house on the Sinclair place. Asa told me about it when I was there. I need to be close to Mama, and I need to get the baby out of here. Please come with me and help me set up a little rural garden center. I told Asa I might bring you, and he said that would be fine. You won't have to do any hard work, just tell me what to do."

Merry Bell just looked at me taking it all in. "Well, that's a lot to think about. I'd have to let this place go or keep on paying rent."

"We can do either one. I can help you make the rent payment, or you can let it go and when you are ready to come back, if you feel that way, I'll help you find something.

"I have to keep him safe, Merry Bell."

"What makes you think he's going to be safer down there in Pete's old territory?"

"I have a plan. Just think about it and let me know by Thursday. I'm going Friday when I get off work. I have to give my notice at the library."

I turned and went back to my room. Neither one of us slept that night. Merry Bell looked out her window at the full moon, as if asking God for the answer. I knew the answer. I just looked over at my sweet child, and I knew. Did I have the strength to go through with it?

# *Epilogue*

What makes a woman give away her child? A child who she wanted from the first day she felt him move—one that she had read her favorite literature to while he was still in the womb, one whose pink cheeks she had kissed a million times.

Her strong love for that child is the only thing that can make this happen. I know there are many people who don't understand why I did what I did.

It's hard for me to look at Asa's now-adult daughter, Lora Sinclair, as I finish my story. We sit on the simple wooden bench in the cemetery where we have a good view of Asa's grave. The iris I planted there are just coming up.

"Finish, Paulette," she says, her eyes demanding more. "Why did you do it?"

I wrap my faded pink cardigan around me more tightly and finish the story—the story she deserves to hear, John, too.

I actually did come here and live in that little house. Merry Bell came with me and helped me plant varieties of flowers that would sell. We also planted a few vegetables.

Soon ladies in town came here to get cut flowers, peas and butterbeans, and finished arrangements. I soon was able to do a pretty good job of designing, and they asked me to come to their homes before a party or special dinner to make the centerpieces. Merry Bell tried to teach me all she had learned over the years in that first month or two.

Not long after I moved in, Asa stopped by to see if we were settling in. He spoke to Merry Bell and then he saw John. He paused mid-sentence and looked past Merry Bell to where the boy was playing with a little brown and white dog who had wandered up and stayed.

"Can I get out and meet him?" he asked.

"Sure."

"Hey there Buddy."

John squinted up at him, but Asa knelt on one knee to be closer to his level.

"Who is your pal there?" he asked, stroking the little dog down his back.

"I don't know his name yet," said John. "What's your name?"

"Asa," he said and gave John a wink.

"Mr. Asa," I corrected. I made myself walk away to tend to some flowers, all the while watching the interaction between them. I could hear Asa talking low and chuckling at things my boy said.

"Look, Buddy, dogs like for you to scratch them behind the ears like this." Asa scratched the dog behind his ear, and the pup seemed to smile and thump his hind foot on the wooden-plank porch, making John giggle.

"Hey, Mr. Asa. My name isn't Buddy. It's John Toliver. Maybe we could name the dog Buddy."

"Hey, great idea. But I need a special name for you. I drive by here at least once a day, and I hope we get to be pals. I'm gonna call you Buckshot. You like that?"

"Yes sir! It sounds like a cowboy name."

Asa shook his hand, gave Buddy a pat, and ambled over to me, his eyes looking down.

When he got to me and looked up, there were tears running down his cheeks.

"Paulette, he's mine, isn't he?"

I silently nodded.

He wiped tears on the sleeve of his denim shirt and sniffed. "Why in the world didn't you tell me?"

"What happened between us was not a passionate love story. You were just being nice to me and trying to get me out of a bad place in my life. We have done fine."

"I can see that. You have done a fine job, you and Merry Bell. Is this why you came back; so I could meet him?" he asked.

The time had come to tell him the truth. But I was afraid of the consequences, like I was afraid to tell Jesse.

"Asa, Pete Lawrence has continued to haunt me. He showed up not far from Merry Bell's house. He threatened me. He thought the baby was his. I knew the minute I held him that he was yours. I found creepy notes on my windshield. I was confronted getting in my car after work.

"I finally convinced him that the baby wasn't his and thought that would be the end of it. But when I got back after visiting Mama, he pulled in the drive way and hinted that he might hurt Merry Bell and take John. He even guessed that John might be yours. I'm sure his motive would be ransom from your family because he knows I don't have any money.

"Jesse hurt Pete pretty bad after he attacked me. Left him with a nasty scar and a blind eye. I was afraid he had killed him. And he would if I told him about this latest incident. I just need to get John around good men, so he will have a role model. We could use a little protection, too."

Asa let all that sink in. His face was red with anger. "I need to think all this through. My wife, Beth, is sick. She has cancer. I don't want to upset her with all this right now."

"I'm so sorry! I had no idea. I don't want you to tell her. She might make more of it than she should. Just let me try to make a go of it here. My promise to you is that I won't make demands on you. Maybe you could let John just tag along some. I'm sure he doesn't like to watch me dig in the dirt all the time."

"I'd love to let him tag along. I just wish I'd known before now. I could have helped you. Anytime things get too hard, I would even raise him.

"I'll make you a deal, a bargain. If you let me see him and love him, I'll never tell him I'm anything more than a special friend. I'll never make him think less of you in any way. And by the way, I named him Buckshot."

"Oh Asa...." Words caught in my throat. I had so much to say and couldn't get a word out.

Asa winked and got in his truck and slowly drove away after waving to John one more time.

The months went by, and I could see that my boy was comfortable with Asa. He stopped and visited him every afternoon. After our discussion, Asa told me not to pay rent and that he would cover utilities. I was barely making enough money for us to live on, and I worked every day all day. By night I was so tired I didn't have the energy to play or read.

"Did you ever hear from Pete after you moved back here?" asked Lora, squinting at me through rays of light coming from behind the old cedars. I didn't realize how long we had been sitting here talking until I felt my legs beginning to go numb.

"I got a few threatening letters. Then after about a year they stopped."

"Do you know why?"

"I could only guess, and again, didn't want to know.

"Back to the story….. By then Merry Bell's bad knee was hurting all the time. She walked with a noticeable limp and wasn't able to help me with the flowers or John. Last year she asked me to find her a place to go where she would be taken care of. It broke my heart that I couldn't be the one to help her. It was my turn.

Little Diana Ross was only four, so I told her that I would keep her and bring her for a visit. I couldn't believe how much had happened since John was born.

In the back of my mind, I felt like I would go back to Tennessee. I found a small retirement home not far from where we had lived.

She was in total agreement and did not want me to be burdened with taking care of her. So, that's what we did. I knew that when I went back I could check on her every day.

I'd have to find a job that payed a real salary, not just a few dollars here and there like I was making with the plants. I'd have to help her with the monthly fee at the home.

I always thought about Asa's words. If he had him, John would have the best male role model and friend. Most importantly, he would be safe.

Occasionally, I still got threatening letters from Pete. Though he never went through with the kidnapping scheme, he always made me look over my shoulder. If John were with Asa, that would stop.

I could leave him for a while, just till he is a little older. I love him too much not to.

By the time John was five, and you were three, I made my move. Your mother had just died. But your extended family included your grandparents, Asa, and your mother's sister Shelly. That gave me the peace of mind that there would be enough people around to love you both and not put the whole burden on Asa.

It was time for the talk.

One day when Asa stopped by, I told him there was something I needed to talk to him about. I reminded him of his bargain, to love John and take care of him if I ever felt like this life was not the right thing for us.

He came in the house and sat in the small living room in an old rocking chair that I had brought from Merry Bell's, staring at the space between his boots.

"What's on your mind?"

I told him. He cried, nodded in agreement, and came over to hug me tenderly.

I knew that I couldn't try to explain the situation to John. He was too little and wouldn't understand. He might cling to me, and then I would melt in a puddle. I told him I had to go check on Merry Bell, which was true, and that he could stay with Asa and play with you. He was excited.

We packed his clothes and his favorite toys and books in a paper sack. As I drove to the house, I felt physically sick. My heart was pounding in my chest.

Buddy came, too, and sat by him on the porch. I told him Asa would be out in just a minute. He reached up and hugged me and gave me a kiss. When I looked back, he smiled happily and waved. Buddy was in his lap.

Out of the corner of my eye, I saw Asa looking out from behind the curtain of one of the tall windows. He gave me a sad wave too.

"Why didn't you try to go back and get Buck?" asked Lora whose eyes were brimming with tears.

I smiled, knowing that was the name she had called him all her life.

"I tried, Lora, several times. One time I just parked a ways from the house and walked up the drive and stopped at that little clump of trees right close to the final curve before you get to the house. I saw Asa and John sitting on the front steps. They were talking and laughing. Buddy was with them, yapping and wagging his tail. They looked so happy."

And there were other times. About six months later, I repeated my attempt, and looked around the corner of the house to see Asa leading John around on his old horse in the wooden pen out back. You were hanging on the lower boards by the toes of your little boots, begging for a turn.

After a few more tries, I gave up. I only

hoped that I could make amends later in life. Thanks to John's new wife, Simsie, for inviting me to their wedding, I've had my chance with both of you.

Asa kept his end of the bargain. He never told John he was his daddy, but I think he must have known. Your daddy may have called it a bargain, but to me, it felt like a promise.

## *Acknowledgements*

The Crossroads Market is not based on any one particular flea market-type event. I was inspired by First Monday Trade Day in Ripley, Miss., which began in 1893. It has taken place every month since. It started as a day set aside once a month for people to come together and trade their wares with others.

www.firstmonday.ripley.ms/history/

My hometown inspiration came from Trade Days, held in Coldwater, Miss., each June, August, and October to benefit the Tate County Rescue Squad. An estimated 360 vendors participate in the flea market.

Oral and written interview with Tim and Jimmy Sanders of Senatobia, long-time flea market vendors.

Many thanks for my proofreaders. It's so hard to write this many words without finding a mistake!

Special thanks to Sara Trotter, my 10th

grade English teacher, who inspired my love of writing and literature. Her guidance continued in helping me edit this book.

And to Howard for his suggestions and for putting up with my absence from everyday life while I finished this book.

As with the first book, Chad Martin with Laurel Rose Publishing made it possible for me to get this book into print.

Book quotations….For the first time in 20 years a large number of works were entered into the Public Domain. Works are in the public domain if they are not covered by intellectual property rights, such as copyright, at all, or if the intellectual property rights to the works has expired.[1] Every work first published before 1923 has been in the American public domain since 1998. Since January 1, 2019, works from 1923 have also lost their copyright protection. After that literature, movies and other works released 96 years ago will enter the public domain every January 1st until 2073. Wikipedia: Public Domain in the United States.

*About the Author*

Nancy Dandridge Patterson, a native Tate Countian, retired after a 37-year career in broadcasting and public relations. She began her career in Mississippi's small-market radio in Holly Springs, Greenwood, and Hernando before joining the staff at Northwest Mississippi Community College's NPR-affiliate station WNJC where she served as manager.

When the station closed in 1988, she transferred to the college's Public Relations Department.

There she won several state and regional awards in feature story writing, photography, layout and design, advertising, and  sports writing in her coverage of the college's rodeo team. She retired in 2010 in her 32nd year at Northwest. The last five years of her career she served as Director of Public Relations.

In retirement, Patterson has continued to write—for area newspapers and magazines. She maintains her personal blog at nonniinbarr.blogspot.com.

A proud alumna of Northwest, Patterson obtained a bachelor's degree from The University of Mississippi in Liberal Arts, with emphases in English, History, Sociology, and Journalism.

Patterson ended a 13-year break from horseback riding in 2015 when she began trail riding. She and her friends ride at local state parks in Mississippi and Tennessee and in the Arkansas Ozark Mountains.

She and her husband, Howard, have three grown children and four grandchildren. They live with their four dogs and two horses on family farmland in North Mississippi.

**Nancy and her Quarter Horse/Appaloosa cross mare ride the trails in Big Flat, Ark. Photo by Mary Hurley**

# Awareness for Cervical Dystonia

Cervical dystonia, also known as spasmodic torticollis, is a rare neurological disorder that originates in the brain. Cervical dystonia is characterized by involuntary muscle contractions in the neck that cause abnormal movements and postures of the neck and head. In some cases, these abnormal contractions may be sustained or continuous; in others, they may be present as spasms that can resemble tremor.

The severity of cervical dystonia can vary, but the disorder can cause significant pain and discomfort as well as difficulty with everyday tasks due to the abnormal postures. It can affect quality of life and activities of daily living including employment. Cervical dystonia typically begins in middle age. The cause of cervical dystonia is unknown, although a genetic susceptibility is thought to underlie some cases.

**National Organization for Rare Disorders**
https://rarediseases.org/rare-diseases/ cervical-dystonia/

I have posted this information here to increase awareness of this rare disorder. There is no cure. Some patients, including me, get relief in the form of botox injections into the neck every three months. Extreme cases can be treated with deep brain stimulation. I'm thankful mine is subtle at this point.

See the color awareness ribbon on the back cover.